Carrion Moon

A BRIG ELLIS TALE

Also by Joe Kilgore

Insomniac: Short Stories for Long Nights

Misfortune's Wake

More Brig Ellis Tales:

Fool's Errand

Cast Them Dead

Carrion Moon

A BRIG ELLIS TALE

JOE KILGORE

Encircle Publications
Farmington, Maine, U.S.A.

To Norman, Pierre, and Irwin

*"Sooner or later everyone sits down
to a banquet of consequences."*

—Robert Louis Stevenson

THE COLONEL HAD TO SHOUT to be heard above the *whop-whop* of the rotors.

"You and your snake eaters ready, Ellis?"

"Born ready, Sir."

"Bang-bangs?"

"Locked and loaded."

"Secret squirrel start to finish, son."

"Zero leaks, Colonel."

"Good. Concerns?"

"Rations? MREs?"

"This is in-and-out. Ammo only. Hot chow when you get back."

"Ten-four."

"Weather's not optimal, but Henderson handles a Black Hawk like his bassinet was a bucket seat."

"Any change in the primary, Colonel?"

"Negative. Bag bandits and bolt."

"Will do, Sir."

"Good hunting, lad."

Ellis snapped to attention and saluted. The Colonel responded in kind, then lowered his head and quickly put distance between himself and the helicopter. Tasso, already seated, offered an arm to help his squad leader aboard. Once Ellis was strapped in, Henderson commenced lift-off and banked the bird into a chillingly black sky.

CHAPTER 1

RAYS OF SUNSHINE BOUNCED OFF the chrome bumper like multiple light flares from photographers' flashbulbs. Of course, photographers seldom used flashbulbs anymore, and chrome bumpers were virtually anachronistic as well. But then so was the car and its driver. The white, 1966 Mercedes 230 SL Convertible was four years shy of being sixty years old, but over the course of decades it had been given lots of new leases on life by enthusiasts of German engineering and design, plus those who favored a bona fide classic over whatever passed for the latest trend. The current owner and driver, Brig Ellis, was one of the latter. At thirty-eight years old he was not into crazes, nor was he one to admire his chariot only on weekends or at car shows. Ellis used it as his main means of transportation. A reasonable income and a reliable mechanic afforded him the wherewithal to keep the beauty mostly out of the shop and on the asphalt, which was particularly agreeable when he was able to put it through its paces on a road trip like his present one.

Top down, aviator sun-shades on, Ellis didn't have to worry about the wind mussing his hair. Even though he had been out of the military for a number of years, he still kept his brown mane close cropped. Living in San Diego provided him a year-round tan so he was unconcerned about sunburn. Nor was he bothered by the temperature change as afternoon segued into evening and twilight began its transition to nightfall.

Ellis was making his way to New Mexico not simply for the inherent joy of guiding a vintage automobile over an impressively stark landscape, but rather for a much more personal reason. The former soldier and current private investigator believed that promises should be kept. And he had made a promise to Tasso.

Ellis joined the Army right out of high school, put in his twenty years, and was now using his military pension to supplement his earnings from what his business card highlighted: INVESTIGATIONS, SECURITY, CONFIDENTIAL MATTERS. Long ago however, he had promised Vic Tasso, one of his former squad members, that if he was still around when the time came, Ellis would make sure Tasso's ashes were returned to the home of his youth in Yavapai County, Arizona. There to be spread among the majestic red rocks of Sedona. The time had come years sooner than he assumed it would, but Ellis hadn't forgotten his commitment. So when authorities found a directive on Tasso's computer as to the native American's wishes upon his demise, Ellis was contacted. Now the San Diego P.I. was on his way to Santa Fe planning to return via Sedona to keep his promise to the indigenous Apache who was, without debate, the best soldier in his old squad.

An ocean of stars spotted the sky as Ellis drove. They lighted the way not only to the task that was before him, but also to the memory that was behind him in what turned out to be his last mission with Tasso, Devlin, Fowler, Adams, and Sanchez. A mission that was supposed to take only a few hours, took a number of days instead—days that deposited themselves permanently into Ellis's memory bank. Some traumatic recollections can be forever locked away so deeply in the inner recesses of the mind that it takes professional help and years of therapy to bring them back to consciousness. This memory was not one of those. This was a memory forever floating on untranquil waters. It could reemerge at the mention of a name, the flicker of a flame, or the request of one of the participants to lay his ashes and soul to rest in the home of his ancestors. This was a memory that gave no sign of ever going away.

THE UH 60 BLACK HAWK helicopter sped through the night sky like a giant dragonfly in midair hunt. Those winged insects give no thought to anything other than the mosquitoes on their menu, but being human, it was impossible for the predators on the Black Hawk to think only of their upcoming prey.

Corporal Sanchez, a stocky twenty-year-old from El Paso by way of Ciudad Juárez, was wondering if his lowrider would still be safe in his uncle's garage when his hitch was up, or was it already being co-opted every weekend by his good-for-nothing cousin? Specialist Devlin, a red-haired Irishman from Brookline, Massachusetts, was praying an imaginary Rosary but keeping his prayers to himself—not wanting to be accused of spooking those around him. Atlanta native, Deets Fowler, was silently crooning Otis Redding's "Dock Of The Bay." It helped him keep his cool until it was time to lose it. Private Adams, Omaha born and reared, was involuntarily bouncing his knees up and down while keeping his boots on deck. Internal nerves made external by the impending mission. Sergeant Victor Tasso, an Apache from the Yavapai reservation near Prescott was checking his equipment and his weapon for the third time. Three's a charm, he believed, and even if it wasn't, the checks would assure he was ready for anything. Lieutenant Brig Ellis was studying each man for signs of something other than full commitment to the task at hand. He saw nothing that concerned him. There was no longer time for worry anyway, they were now only five miles from the landing zone.

"Goggles on," Ellis barked.

The black night quickly turned green as each man activated his PVS-14. All superfluous thoughts vanished from each soldier's head as their senses locked in on what they were there to do.

Warrant Officer Henderson leaned toward Ellis and said, "Under three, Lieutenant."

Ellis turned to Tasso and simply nodded.

The Apache released his restraint, squatted, and one by one looked each man in the eye while gripping his shoulder. One, two, three, four affirmative head nods. They were ready.

Henderson spoke. "L Z dead ahead, Lieutenant." Then he began to guide the bird down. One hundred feet. Fifty feet. Twenty-five. Ten. Touch down."

With something approaching severe understatement, Henderson said to Ellis, "Guess I don't have to tell you to make it snappy, huh?"

"Just keep the meter running, Warrant Officer. We'll be back before you know it."

CHAPTER 2

'WE'LL BE BACK BEFORE YOU know it.' Ellis's words still caught in his throat. But he managed to put those words and thoughts away for the time being as he steered the Mercedes around a bend spotted with hedgehog cactus and in the distance, the lights of Santa Fe.

Hotel Chimayo was just off the central plaza in Old Town. It wasn't cheap but it wasn't nearly as pricey as the Inn of the Anasazi right next door or the fabled La Fonda at the corner. Ellis didn't need to pinch pennies but he wasn't into extravagance either. Chimayo was right in the heart of things and while definitely dated, it was still comfortable. It also allowed him to park his own car in their basement garage, which was actually the incentive that cemented his decision.

After checking in and dropping his gear in his room, Ellis decided to stretch his legs. It had been a thirteen hour drive and even though he had stopped occasionally for gas and snacks along the way, there were still a lot of muscles quietly asking to be unkinked. After strolling by a number of galleries, restaurants, clothing stores, coffee shops, and more, Ellis decided to return via the plaza. At ten p.m. there were still a number of people in the park, tourists mostly, Ellis assumed. He passed families, couples, a young guy smoking, and a woman with a dog. The canine put him in mind of his own pooch, Osgood, the English bulldog. Ellis assumed that at this time of night the four-legged meatloaf was probably snoring loudly in one of the pens at the pet hotel the P.I. always used when he had to go out of town. Probably good that he hadn't brought him along, Ellis thought. Osgood might have been a little too attracted to the woman's Shih Tzu. The bruiser was an incorrigible lady's man.

A nightcap seemed in order when Ellis got back to Chimayo. He found the hotel's watering hole just off the lobby, stepped inside and took a stool at the bar. Behind it, a petite, short-haired brunette was drying glasses and slipping them back into their regimented formations. Without even turning around to look at him, she said, "What can I get you?"

"Woodford Reserve, neat," he answered.

Never missing a beat, she took the bottle from the shelf, poured the bourbon, turned and put it in front of him, saying "Wise choice."

"A function of trial and error," he quipped. "Lots of error."

"It's not where you start, it's where you finish," she replied. "My name's Bevel."

"Bevel? That's an interesting name. But it sounds like kind of an old moniker for such a young woman."

"Almost everyone I know agrees. So, most just call me Bev."

"Well, I'd like to call you Bevel. It suits you. I can see a well-traveled soul behind those sparkling brown eyes."

"Wow, that's a new one. You one of those visiting Hollywood types we get a lot of around here. A writer maybe?"

"Right state, wrong town and occupation," Ellis said, pulling a business card from his shirt pocket and setting it down on the bar.

She read it and said, "Brig, huh? And you're talking smack about my name?"

"Got a point there. Most folks just call me Ellis."

"Well, I'd like to call you Brig, like the navy jailhouse. Behind those sad green eyes, I see a cell in your past… or maybe it's in your future."

"Like to make up stories about your patrons, do you?"

"Not all of them. Just the ones who tell me my brown eyes sparkle."

"Well, they do. And I thought you should know it. But what's with my eyes being sad? Where'd that come from?"

"Actually from your business card. I just assumed anyone who does what you do for a living must have had some tough times in his past."

"Doesn't everyone?"

"Everyone I know," Bevel answered.

"Me, too," Ellis replied. "Why don't you come around again with that Woodford, and I'll buy you one, if you like."

"I do like, but we're not supposed to drink with the customers."

Ellis twisted on his stool, looked around, and saw that he and Bevel were the only ones there. "Tell you what, I won't mention it to your employer if you don't."

"Deal," she said, pulling a glass from the shelf beneath the bar, replenishing his, and pouring one for herself.

"What should we drink to?" he asked.

"I don't know. Which is it?"

"Which is what?"

"Like it says on your business card… Investigation, Security, or Confidential Matters?"

"Well, it's really none of the three. Just in town to see an old friend of mine."

"Male or female?"

"Male."

"Young or old?"

"Too young to be in his current condition."

"And what condition might that be?"

"Dead."

"Oh," she said. And added sincerely. "I'm very sorry. I had no idea."

"Nothing to be sorry about. Happens to everyone eventually."

"Was he… a very good friend?"

"He was… a long time ago. A good friend. A good man."

"Let's drink to him, then," Bevel said. "What is… I mean what was his name?"

"Victorio Tasso. Vic for short. But not for long enough, as it turned out."

She clinked her glass against Ellis's and said, "To Vic!"

"To Vic," he answered, and they both drank.

"Want to talk about him?"

"Not really," Ellis replied. "Might make my sad eyes sadder."

"Can't have that. Next one's on the house. Then we can get back to flirting."

"Damn, is that what we were doing? Why am I always the last to know?"

"The last to know what, dickhead?"

Neither the voice nor the sentiment came from Bevel. It came from a short block of granite in a western style suit. His powder blue attire was as offensive as his remark, which was immediately followed by a question just as provocative.

"This asshole giving you a hard time, Bev?"

Ellis couldn't believe the mouth on this five-foot eight inch anvil. But it had been a long day. He stayed silent and sipped his bourbon.

Addressing the late arrival, Bevel said, "Don't be such an insufferable prick, Clifford. Where the hell do you get off waltzing in here and insulting one of our guests?"

"Guest gets out-of-line with you, babe, you know I'll put a stop to it."

"I'm not your babe. And he's not the one that's out-of-line, Clifford. That would be you. Now apologize to the man, order something, or get the hell out of here. On second thought, why not just go with that last option."

"I didn't mean to upset you, Bev. I just worry about you working these hours when who-knows-what might stagger in here."

"He didn't stagger and he didn't come in as a braying jackass… like some people I know."

"Well," the flustered boulder said, "I just didn't like the way he was looking at you."

Bevel sighed and put both hands on the bar. "I cannot believe you are still doing this two years later. What do you not understand about the word, divorced?"

"I've always kind of thought of it as sort of a trial separation, you know?"

"No, I don't know." The flustered barmaid barked. "But if you want to think of it as a trial separation, well, the damn trial is over with, you were convicted, and we are definitely separated for good. Got it?"

Ellis was silently regretting this end to a very long day. Ordinarily, he would have just paid his tab and walked out. But he wasn't sure he should leave Bevel alone with the lout.

"Brig, I'm really sorry about this. My ex-husband… emphasis on the ex… has obviously had a few too many before coming in here. But he's not staying. Are you Clifford?"

"So that's it. You want to be alone with him. That's why you want me out, right? Should have expected as much from a slut like you."

That was one step too far. Ellis turned from his drink and spoke to the oaf.

"You know… Clifford, is it? You know, Clifford, when you call me names, well that's one thing. Lots of people call me lots of names. I'm used to it. But when you insult Bevel, and spew your venom her way, well frankly, that's just too much. I'm afraid you're going to have to leave now."

"Me leave? You going to make me? Ha! I can break your scrawny ass in half. Do you know I can bench press 500 pounds?"

Ellis knew he shouldn't do what he was about to do, but the last thing he wanted was a bar fight after a thirteen hour drive. So he said, "No, I didn't know that you can bench press 500 pounds." Then Ellis reached inside his jacket. When his hand came back out, it wasn't empty. "But did you know, sitting right here, I can actually lift this Glock 19 with a full clip."

Nothing sobers one quicker or focuses the mind sharper than having a gun barrel staring you in the face. That's certainly the dual affect it had on Clifford as Ellis continued to speak.

"Do you have any idea what it feels like to have a round go through your kneecap? Then, on top of all that pain, you become a cripple for the rest of your life. Of course, I could go up and right a little bit and change you from a bellowing baritone into a trembling tenor. Or… you could just keep your mouth completely shut, walk out of here right now, go home, and go to bed… without having bone, blood, and blubber all over that ridiculous suit."

Stunned silence and the look on Clifford's face made it obvious to Bevel and Ellis that Clifford was definitely going with the last option. He immediately exited the bar even more quickly and much more quietly than he had entered. When they were alone again, Ellis asked, "He's not going to come at you later, is he?"

"No," Bevel said, assuredly. "I'm sure if he hasn't wet his pants already, he soon will. Never seen him that scared before."

"You were married to that guy?" Ellis asked.

"Hey we all mistakes. Some are just more stupid than others. Clifford was the stupidest."

"Well, sounds like you knew when to cut bait."

"Yep. Got the divorce decree. Guess a restraining order of some sort is warranted."

"Can't hurt," Ellis acknowledged. "Lets him know even the law thinks he's a doofus. Maybe eventually it will sink in."

"Maybe."

"Been a long day," Ellis said, "Have to stay at it much longer?"

"Naw," she replied. "Night manager lets me close up early when it's slow like this."

Taking a pen from his pocket, Ellis wrote his room number on the business card he had put on the bar. "Charge the drinks to the room, okay?"

"Okay," Bevel said. Then putting one hand on top of his, she said, "Thanks for dealing with that. Wish I could show you how much I really appreciate it."

"Why do you think I put the room number on the card?"

THE MISSION…

"TO THE TREE LINE," ELLIS said, "go!"

Tasso led the way as the squad tumbled out of the helicopter and dashed into the nearby wood. Ellis brought up the rear. As each member scrambled beneath the cover of foliage and darkness, Tasso would point left or right indicating where he wanted each man. When Ellis reached the Sergeant he knelt and checked his compass coordinates. Then he rose to a crouch and began making his way through the thick underbrush. Tasso motioned for each soldier to move out and follow their Lieutenant. Initially he stayed at the back, but as they progressed the Apache picked up his pace and began to pass the others until only Ellis remained in front of him.

Forward movement was constant but labored. Limbs, leaves, vines, and tree trunks provided concealment but also hindered speed. Ellis knew the mission's operational tempo was fast and faster, so he kept the pace as rapid as possible. Slogging through both over-and-undergrowth taxed the soldiers' stamina. Though each was in superb physical condition, the stale air and lack of any mollifying breeze, along with the intense humidity, caused them to sweat profusely. Yet no man was allowing the elements or his body's involuntary responses to slow him down. Adrenalin was the antidote to fatigue.

After fifteen minutes of double-timing through the thickness that enfolded them, the squad reached a clearing not carved by God but cut by man. The open ground encircled a house rimmed only by a five foot retaining wall. No lights shone inside the building. No guards were visible around the perimeter. Pausing momentarily to assess the situation, Ellis motioned for Tasso to take Sanchez and Devlin and approach from the right while he'd lead Fowler and Adams in from the left. Scampering across the divide, both teams reached the retaining wall at the same time. Ellis swung himself over and crouched low on the other side. Tasso did the same. Weapons ready, each kept watch as the others came over the wall behind them.

Once again, it appeared no sentries had been posted. The Americans fanned out and on Ellis's hand signal they all darted to the house. With their backs against the wall, Ellis made sure that Tasso could see him. Following pre-arranged plans, he gave one deep head-nod. Tasso took his half of the squad to the back while Ellis and his mates scurried to the front. Beside the door now, Ellis reached out and tried to turn the knob. It was locked. He motioned to Fowler who quickly swung around him and placed a small charge at the base of the door then flattened himself against the wall on the entryway's opposite side. The explosion would be the signal for Tasso and the two men with him to breach from the rear. Ellis counted to five slowly. Then he pushed the release that fired the detonator inserted in the charge. The shock wave blew the door to hell and gone.

CHAPTER 3

ELLIS HAD FINISHED HIS MORNING run, plus his shower, and had only a towel around him as he was about to shave. The knock at the door kept him from squeezing the foam into his hand. "Yes?" He yelled from the bathroom and waited for a reply. The knocking continued. "Who is it?"

"Santa Fe Police Department," came the reply. "You need to let us in."

"Just a minute," Ellis said loudly as he removed the towel, threw it over the shower curtain rod and stepped into the main room. He quickly pulled underwear from his overnight bag, slipped the shorts on, followed quickly by his pants.

"Mr. Ellis?"

"Coming," he answered, as he pulled a T-shirt over his head while walking to the door. He then opened it, still in his bare feet.

"Are you Brig Ellis?"

"I am. Who are you?"

"I'm Detective Ordona with the Santa Fe Police Department," the officer said, holding out his badge for Ellis to inspect. The P.I. gave it and the man clutching it a once-over. The badge looked official and the man serious. Standing directly behind him was another individual both taller and wider and seemingly just as solemn. "This is Officer Wilcrest.

If you'd like to see his—"

"That won't be necessary," Ellis said, opening the door wide enough for the two men to come in. "What can I do for you?"

Ordona asked, "Are you alone, Mr. Ellis?"

"I am."

"Could we see some identification, please?"

"Sure," Ellis said, taking his wallet off the bureau and opening it to reveal his Private Detective License. He handed it to Ordona.

The policeman reviewed it, then handed it back.

"What can I—"

Before Ellis could complete his sentence, Ordona spoke again. "Do you have a weapon with you, Mr. Ellis?"

"I do. Not on me. But here in the room. And before you ask, I also have a permit to carry."

"A New Mexico permit?"

"No. California."

"Would you be kind enough to show Officer Wilcrest where the weapon is? We'd like to see the permit as well."

Ellis pulled a folded copy of his conceal-carry permit from his wallet and was about to open the drawer to get the Glock when Ordona interjected.

"If the weapon is in the drawer, please let Officer Wilcrest retrieve it. Wouldn't want any behavior misconstrued."

"Nor would I." Ellis said. "Top drawer, Officer Wilcrest. Be my guest."

The silent, burly policeman opened the drawer, looked inside, then took a pen from his pocket. He inserted the pen between the trigger and the finger guard, then proceeded to drop the Glock into a plastic bag he had, up to that point, kept unseen.

"Is all this really necessary?" Ellis asked.

Ordona ignored the question and asked, "Do you know a man named Clifford James, Mr. Ellis?"

"I'm not sure."

"Not sure? Either you do or you don't," Ordona replied.

"I believe I did meet a fellow in the bar last night. And now that you mention it, the name Clifford came up. But I don't know if that was his first name or last."

"You and Mr. James have words?"

"Well, if we're talking about the same fellow, he was drunk, Detective. Foul mouthed too. Began to get verbally abusive with the barmaid."

"And what did you do about that?"

"I convinced him that he ought to leave."

"How did you do that?"

"Got a feeling you already know," Ellis began. "Look, Detective Ordona, it was late, I was tired, and he was being a world-class prick to the woman behind the bar. I didn't want to get into a physical altercation with him… which he appeared intent upon. I know I shouldn't have, but I used my piece to frighten him. Just to get him to leave. I never had any intention of using it."

Ordona didn't miss a beat. "He said you threatened his life?"

"False. I merely pointed out to him the wisdom of departing."

"Well, after he departed, he came to the police station and filled out a report. Accusing you of brandishing a gun and threatening to kill him."

"And you believed him? You couldn't tell he was heavily intoxicated?"

"I wasn't there. The duty officer took the complaint."

"Well, that officer must have noted his condition, and

questioned the veracity of his claim. Or I would have been visited from someone in your department soon afterward, correct?"

"That's partially correct. The duty officer had misgivings. And Mr. James didn't have your name."

"Then how did you know to come to me?"

"We checked with the front desk for charges in the bar last night. The final ones were made to you… at a time that would have shortly preceded Mr. James's arrival at our station."

"Detective, chances are the guy has sobered up by now," Ellis began. "Probably realizes he was plastered and made a fool of himself. Bet he wishes he hadn't lodged a complaint with you guys. Why not just check with him and see if he doesn't want to drop the whole thing?"

"Can't do that," Ordona replied. "Last night… actually, very early in the morning hours… Clifford James's body was found just outside the city limits. He's dead."

Less than a second of silence elapsed before Ellis said, "I'm sorry. Hate to hear that. Cause of death?"

"The coroner's looking into that now."

"Well, listen. I certainly had nothing to do with it. Check my weapon, you'll find it hasn't been fired for some time."

"Didn't say he was shot. Didn't say he wasn't."

"Then why bag my Glock?"

"As far as we know, you were one of the last people to see him alive before he came to the station. He told the duty officer you pointed a gun at him. You confirmed as much. Officer Wilcrest and I don't like walking into situations where a gun may be pointed at us. We're cautious that way."

"All right, fine, but—"

"Mr. Ellis, did you leave the hotel last night after you left the bar?"

"No. I didn't."

"How can we confirm that?"

"You're asking me? You're the policeman."

"Even an older hotel like this one has security video, you know."

"Good," Ellis responded. "Then you'll probably see when I drove my car in the building garage. And you'll see that I never drove it out."

"We did see that," Ordona said. "We also saw when you left the lobby last night by the main entrance, then later returned."

"I took a walk after I arrived. That's the only time I left until my run this morning."

"The tape also shows you leaving and returning from your run. But management acknowledges there's not a camera covering every possible exit."

"Well, that's too bad. But the fact is, I didn't leave all night."

"Anyway to verify that?"

"What do you mean?"

"Simple question. Can anyone, other than yourself, verify that you stayed in the hotel all night?"

Ellis's pause was a bit too pregnant for Ordona to miss.

"Did you spend the night alone?"

Ellis didn't want to bring the woman into the conversation, but he also didn't want to be caught lying to police where a death was involved.

"No. I wasn't alone. There was a young lady here until early this morning. She left just before I went for a run."

"Then she can provide you with an alibi, I assume."

"Well, yes… she could. But is there really any need?"

"There is. What's her name," Ordona asked, pulling a pen and pad out of his jacket.

"It's… Bevel," Ellis said.

"That a first name or last?"

"First."

"And the last is?"

Ellis hesitated momentarily. "Not really certain." Then he thought, *hell, they're going to find out one way or another anyway.* "It could be… James."

Ordona's head never moved, but his eyes rose from the pad to the P. I.'s face."

"Yeah," Ellis said sheepishly, "she's his ex-wife."

The previously silent Officer Wilcrest uttered his first word, "Damn."

"Let me see if I have this straight," Ordona began. "You arrive in Santa Fe, check into the hotel, go for a walk, return to the bar, engage a married woman—"

"Ex-married woman," Ellis cut in.

"You engage a woman in conversation, threaten her former husband with a loaded weapon, subsequently take the woman to bed, and her ex-husband winds up dead. Is that about it?"

"Well, it's missing a good bit of nuance, Detective."

"This is New Mexico, Mr. Ellis. We deal in facts. We'll leave the nuance to you Californians. And frankly, the facts put you in a pretty bad light."

"I'm sure when you speak to Ms.… to Bevel, she'll confirm what I told you. But go easy, okay. I mean, well, you know how it is."

"Actually, I don't. I've been married for quite some time."

"The point is… sometimes these things just happen. Totally unplanned. Two consenting adults. Where's the harm?"

"The harm is all over Mr. James's dead body. More than enough harm to go around. I suppose it's purely coincidence that you… and this Bevel… will be able to provide alibis for one another."

"Look, Detective, I'm not a fan of coincidence either, but in this instance, what I told you is the truth."

"Why are you in Santa Fe, Mr. Ellis?

"I'm here to do a favor for a friend."

"And the friend's name would be…?"

"Victor Tasso."

Again the police detective stopped writing. "I assume you know Victor Tasso is also recently deceased."

"Of course, I know. That's why I'm here. We were in the service together some time ago. When we mustered out, he asked that if he died before me, would I see to it that his remains were returned to Arizona where he grew up. I told him I would. That's the only reason I'm here. To pick up his ashes and take them back there."

Ordona's countenance remained blank as he asked, "Are you aware of how Victor Tasso died?"

"No. I didn't receive any details about that. Just that he had died and been cremated and that information was found on his computer asking that I be contacted. I was planning on going to the mortuary after breakfast this morning."

"Well, when you do," Ordona said, "you'll likely learn that Victor Tasso ostensibly died from blood loss due to wounds inflicted by assailant or assailants as yet unknown."

"Assailants? You mean Vic was killed? How?"

"Couldn't be determined to a certainty."

"What?"

"There was considerable blood loss caused by injuries to his extremities and torso. Savage injuries that appear to have been inflicted by teeth and claws."

"Wild animals? That's strange," Ellis said. "Vic was one of the best hunters I know."

"What makes you assume he was hunting?"

"The type of injuries you mentioned. I just assumed he was found in the countryside."

"That's true. But no rifle, shotgun, or other weapon was located. Could have been hiking, communing with nature as the saying goes, or any number of things. What was left of his clothes and footwear looked casual. Boots he had on could have been used for hiking. Hard to say."

Ellis asked, "Who found him?"

"Couple of hunters."

"Did Vic have a car, or truck? Was it nearby?"

"Only vehicle registered to him was at his residence."

"And you're positive it was animals?"

"Animals were definitely involved. Outside the city limits there are all kinds. Bear, mountain lion, and some that travel in packs. Coyotes. Wolves."

Ellis paused before asking his next question. He wasn't sure he really wanted to know the answer. "Know whether he died before or after the animals…"

"Medical examiner said it was difficult to tell. Too much damage inflicted. Too long before the body was actually found. Too many parts missing."

"Jesus," Ellis grunted.

"Scavengers aren't picky eaters."

"Can't stand the idea of a good guy like Vic going that way."

"By the way, Mr. Ellis," Ordona said, while checking back through his notepad, "where were you three or four weeks ago, specifically around April eighth or ninth?"

"Don't have the slightest idea, detective. I'd have to check my calendar which is back in my office in San Diego."

"You didn't happen to come to Santa Fe for any reason around then, did you?"

"No. Why would you ask me that?"

"Can you prove where you were on the days I mentioned?"

The way Tasso died was a shock. The questions Ordona was asking were puzzling. Ellis's frustration meter was getting seriously close to red-lining.

"I told you I don't specifically know where I was then. I'd have to check. But I was definitely in San Diego and not Santa Fe. Why would you even ask a question like that?"

"I ask because your first so-called coincidence is that you were banging the most recent victim's ex-wife. The second coincidence is that you're acquainted with not one, but two victims of violent death. And then there's the fact that Clifford James's body displayed the same type of horrific mauling as Tasso's. Three coincidences, Mr. Ellis? What are the odds?"

SMOKE AND HAZE RIMMED THE gaping crater where the front door had been. No lights illuminated the darkness, but with night goggles crystallizing everything around them, Ellis, Fowler, and Adams burst inside, each assuming search-and-destroy positions. Tasso, Sanchez, and Devlin blew the back door and entered from the rear. There was no need for orders. Each man had already received specific instructions that any individual inside the house was a combatant to be dispatched upon contact. The first was a bearded fat man on a lumpy couch. He barely had time to jump up and rub his eyes before Fowler's Heckler and Koch carbine riddled his chest. Adams got the second as the hostile wandered blindly into the room waving a machete until three M4a1 rounds slammed him against the wall. Ellis began ascending the front stairway. He heard movement before he saw the man with glasses lean over the top rail, Kalashnikov in hand. The Lieutenant's single shot to the forehead took the would-be defender out.

While the front team was advancing, the rear guard was covering the back staircase. Three men in nightshirts burst out of two of the bedrooms and started down. Tasso's burst felled all three. Sanchez and Devlin raced up the stairs to make sure they were finished while the Apache Sergeant kept watch below. Bursts to the heads of the fallen eliminated any potential for last-second retribution.

Ellis entered a room where he found a tall man in underwear sitting on the side of the bed. One of his hands was raised as if he were surrendering, the other was under his pillow. There was no time for debate or discussion, Ellis put a bullet through his heart. Then he walked over, tossed the pillow, and saw a forty-five automatic still clutched in the dead man's hand.

A final room upstairs was yet to be cleared. Sanchez and Devlin were on one side of the door with Fowler and Adams on the other. Sanchez kicked it open and hit the deck. Fowler stepped over him just in time to see a bare ass go out the second floor window. "Runner!" the Black soldier shouted. Devlin repeated even louder so Tasso would hear him below. "Runner!"

The Apache bolted. He raced through the kitchen and tore out through the hole where the back door had been. The naked man was making a mad dash for the retaining wall. Tasso didn't hesitate. He aimed, fired, and dropped the fleeing nude in mid-stride.

Adams was about to check the closet in the last room when he heard whimpering on the other side of the door. "Fellas," he said, "there's somebody in there and it doesn't sound like a guy."

"Lock on it," Sanchez said. Then he stepped back and joined the others who trained their weapons dead center. Adams stood to the side, gripped the knob and quickly swung the door open.

They all saw her at the same time. A skinny, wild-haired adolescent cowering on her haunches in the back of the closet with only a ratty T-shirt to cover her.

"*Ha i kufsan. Ha i kufsan.*" She moaned.

"What the hell's she saying?" Devlin asked.

Sanchez answered. "I think it's, 'Don't rape me. Don't rape me.'"

"You know the orders," Fowler said.

Sanchez turned from the kid to his compatriots saying, "Yeah, but she's only—"

He didn't have time to finish. The girl sprung from her crouched position in a leap. Her hand, which had been against the wall and unseen, now held a paring knife. She ferociously plunged it into the back of Sanchez's neck. Fowler immediately stuck the barrel of his weapon against the girl's temple and pulled the trigger. Splatter from the exit wound covered the back wall of the closet like a Jackson Pollock fresco.

CHAPTER 4

THE DRIVE FROM ELLIS'S HOTEL to Perpetual Rest Mortuary took only fifteen minutes, but all of those minutes were filled with questions bouncing around the private investigator's brain like a pinball careening into and off of one obstacle after another. Ping! How could a master of the wild like Tasso let some beast get the best of him? Ping! Why didn't he have a weapon with him? Ping! If his vehicle was at his home, how did he get where they found him? Ping! Ping! Ping! And what was the deal with two different bodies, his and Bevel's ex, being similarly ripped to shreds?

Detective Ordona had not provided any additional information or increased the hassle factor before he and Officer Wilcrest left with Ellis's Glock. The policeman could have compounded the complaint that the now-deceased Clifford James had made. He could have charged the P.I. for taking his weapon into a venue that served alcohol, but instead he told Ellis he'd just hold onto the piece for safe keeping until the San Diego resident was ready to leave Santa Fe. Ellis had initially planned to leave as soon as he picked up Tasso's remains. Now he wasn't so sure. One more day might be worthwhile. He wanted answers to those questions that continued to ping.

The Perpetual Rest Mortuary was a one-story building on the north side of the city. Unlike many of the adobe buildings throughout Santa Fe, this one was white brick with a large portico in front supported by columns that made it look stately as well as subdued. Of course, like most edifices in its industry, the front was meant to show respectful restraint, the middle was for friends to grieve and relatives to select caskets or urns, while the back housed the more utilitarian functions of cremation and embalming. One stop shopping on the way out life's door.

In the parking lot, Ellis sat in his car momentarily before going inside. In addition to the pinging questions he had about Tasso's demise, he also had pangs of guilt for having lost touch with the Apache and their other squad members he shared such turbulent times with. When you go through one dangerous situation after another together, you feel you're going to be mates forever, Ellis reflected. But eventually you opt out, say your goodbyes, and promise to stay in touch. Then before you know it, time and distance have put enough world between you that you seldom give a second thought to people you fought to keep alive—people who did the same for you. Life moves inexorably on. Until one day it doesn't. Then you have to wonder whether all that living between then and now really meant anything or not. Or whether the only thing that truly mattered was what you did when you were continually focused on trying to keep each other alive. Jesus, Ellis said to himself. *What the hell am I going on about. Just get out of the damn car and get on with it.* So he did.

"May I help you, Sir?" The question came from a five-foot, five-inch garden gnome in a charcoal suit with matching tie.

"I'm here to pick up a friend," Ellis said.

"I'm afraid you and I are the only ones here at the moment."

"No. What I meant was I'm here to pick up… the remains of a friend."

"Oh, of course you are. How silly of me. And where are my manners? Let me introduce myself. I'm Raymond Kershaw," he said, offering his hand, "one of the directors here."

Ellis responded while shaking the man's hand, "My name is Brig Ellis."

"And who is the dearly departed you're here for?"

"Victor Tasso."

"Oh yes, Mr. Tasso. I remember now. What an unfortunate situation. We were informed that he had left instructions. Could you follow me, please?"

The little man led the way down a hallway then stepped through the open door of an office on his right. "Please, have a seat," he said, motioning to one of two chairs that fronted a desk he sat behind.

"Now," Kershaw began, turning to his computer. "Let me just pull up the appropriate information."

Ellis watched the man's stubby little fingers poking the keyboard as he asked, "Did you know Mr. Tasso?"

"No, we had never met him personally."

"Any reason that you can think of that would explain why he chose your establishment for his…"

"It's my understanding that Mr. Tasso made no specific requests regarding where he would be prepared. The police simply informed us that their investigation found that cremation had been desired and that a family friend… let's see, yes, Mr. Brig Ellis… which, of course, would be you… would be coming to claim Mr. Tasso. By the way, simply protocol you know, but could I see some identification, please?"

"Sure," Ellis responded, reaching for his wallet and pulling his driver's license out as he spoke. "You mentioned the word family a moment ago. Do you know if Vic, I mean Mr. Tasso, do you know if he had any family or friends here? Has anyone come by to ask about him?"

"I'm not aware of anyone, no. Thank you," Kershaw said, handing the license back.

"If Mr. Tasso didn't actually request that your organization be involved…?"

"Like others in our business, we have a contract with the city. When someone passes and there's no one or no specific directions, we are one of the establishments that provide appropriate services."

"I see."

"Now, as to a vessel," Kershaw began, spreading out a color brochure in front of Ellis. "As you can see—"

Ellis quickly cut him off. "I don't really need anything like that. You see I'm just transporting the ashes to—"

"Are they to be interred? If so—"

"They're to be scattered."

"Still, I'm sure in memory of your friend…"

Ellis didn't really want to have a conversation about urns. Neither did he want to be taken. He didn't think Tasso would care one way or the other. But he didn't want to disrespect a man he had fought beside either. "Uh, that one. How much is that one?"

"Ah yes, our Lenox Oaktree model. Poplar wood and bronze. Practical but contemporary."

"How much is that?"

"Two hundred and forty-five dollars… plus tax."

"Fine. I'll take that one."

Kershaw knew when to take yes for an answer. "It will be just a moment while I secure things. Can I get you a coffee while you wait?"

"No. I'm fine. Let's just get this done, okay?"

"Certainly," the gnome nodded. "I understand how trying this can be. I'll be back momentarily."

Kershaw left the office. Ellis stood, then went round to the other side of the desk so he could scan the computer monitor. A form was displayed with pertinent information about Victor Tasso. Name. Address. Employer. Etc. Ellis pulled the top sheet off Kershaw's notepad and jotted down what he wanted. Then he took the same chair he had been seated in before and waited for the funeral director to return with what remained of his friend. When he did, the duos' parting was amicable but swift.

On his way to Tasso's former address, Ellis had to admit that the six-inch long by ten-inch wide wooden container was appropriately understated. Much like his old mate, it didn't go out of its way to let people know what it was. The P.I. felt a bit odd about locking it in the trunk of his car, but it seemed the right thing to do. At least it would be safely tucked away while he perused the deceased's apartment. Somehow it didn't seem proper to have a box full of human remains along if one happened to get pinched while breaking and entering.

The door to Tasso's apartment was locked but Ellis carried a Bogata Rake in his inside breast pocket for just such occasions. He used the tool's peaks and valleys to manipulate the lock and let himself inside. Even though it had been a number of weeks since his friend's death, it appeared that the place was probably pretty much as he left it. No one had come yet to box things and take it all away so the apartment could be prepared for the next occupant. Who does that, Ellis wondered, and what's to be done with everything that's left behind? Especially if the one who's left it all is primarily a loner, as Tasso appeared to be. Ellis peeked in closets and opened drawers but found nothing to indicate anyone other than a single male occupied the premises. No second toothbrush in the bathroom, no panties in the laundry basket, not even any condoms in the drawer of the bedside table. Ellis had no idea what kind of life Tasso had been living but apparently it wasn't one of unbridled hedonism. From what he remembered of his friend, he never assumed it would be. He did find a framed photo of what the men in the picture used to call The Last Squad. The last squad to bitch about assignments. The last squad to quit the fight. The last squad standing no matter what. That was how Tasso, Sanchez, Devlin, Fowler, and Adams felt about themselves. Pride was etched on their faces in the photograph, and embedded in Ellis's heart for once having led them.

After leaving the apartment, Ellis went to The Shadow Gallery on Canyon Road. It had been listed as Tasso's current employer when he was killed. The place was filled with Native American oil paintings, sculptures, designer jewelry, and objets d'art. The owner told him that Tasso didn't create any of the work, but that he had a keen interest and appreciation in all of the pieces and proved himself a worthy representative of the art and the gallery. He also confided that Tasso's physical features—black hair, high cheekbones, lined forehead and hawk nose—frequently contributed to his ability to interest browsers. The proprietor couldn't really tell Ellis anything about Tasso's personal life, saying that the Apache chose to keep that to himself. When asked if there had ever been any sort of disagreement or conflict with any of the gallery's customers, nothing sprang to mind. Though he did recall an incident that occurred a few days before Tasso's body was found. A man had been browsing in the front of the gallery while Tasso was helping another customer in the back. When Tasso saw the man, he immediately left the customer he was helping and started toward him. The man saw Tasso heading his way and abruptly left through the front door. Tasso actually followed him outside. He returned only a few minutes later and made no mention of the encounter. When the owner, after helping the customer that Tasso had abandoned, asked him about it, Tasso simply said he had mistaken the man for someone else. The Tasso that Ellis had known, however, didn't make those kind of mistakes.

"ANYONE HURT," ELLIS ASKED.

Fowler answered, "That ISIS whore stabbed Sanchez."

It was then Ellis noticed the handle of the knife protruding from the back of the corporal's neck.

"Damn. How long is the blade?

"Only got a quick look, but no more than two and a half, three inches, maybe," Fowler said.

"Blood loss?"

Adams chimed in, "Minimal, Lieutenant. Almost non-existent."

Ellis turned from Fowler to Sanchez. "How do you feel, Corporal?"

Sanchez replied quickly. "Okay, sir. Neck's a little sore. Hurts a bit when I try to move it from side to side." He reached up to grab the back of his neck but Devlin caught his arm and held it.

"Feel like you can walk?"

"Affirmative, sir."

"Okay, we leave it in for now. Don't want to start a lot of bleeding if we don't have to. Need to get back to the bird. Fowler, you stay behind Sanchez. Let me know if anything changes. I'll take point. Tasso, you're rear. Corporal, let us know if you start to feel bad, weak, or anyway other than hard core."

"Just feel like getting out of here, Lieutenant."

"Okay then. Let's go."

The way out was as unencumbered as the way in. They crossed the courtyard without incident. Each went over the retaining wall in turn. Sanchez grimaced a bit, but he didn't slow down. They entered the tree line single file, heading back via the route they used coming in. Branches and small limbs were pushed aside as they double-timed. Devlin was in front of Sanchez and did what he could to hold the foliage back so the corporal didn't have to jerk his neck to avoid being smacked. Space between the fleeing soldiers started to increase, but Tasso wouldn't let the line get too long. He made sure everyone kept up the pace.

As they approached the clearing they could hear the rotors before seeing the helicopter. At the woods' edge Ellis stopped. He looked back to make sure the rest of the squad was closing. He knew they were ready to make their break when he saw Tasso give his hand signal that everyone was accounted for. He was about to turn and break for the clearing when a white hot tracer hit the Blackhawk and burst it into a blazing fireball. The strike lit up the night like Boston harbor on the fourth of July and blew Ellis and the squad members back on their asses.

Shock and silence reigned momentarily. Then Devlin said, "Lieutenant, that wasn't our ride, was it?"

Ellis answered, "'Was' is the operative word, Specialist."

CHAPTER 5

ELLIS LEFT THE GALLERY AND returned to the hotel. After parking his car, he took the urn from the trunk. Somehow it didn't feel right leaving it in there. He went back to the lobby and crossed to the bar to see if Bevel was on duty. She was. He entered, took a stool, and sat the container on the empty seat beside him.

"Is that what I think it is," she asked.

"Yes. My friend, Vic Tasso. I'm going to take him up to the room with me."

"Thought you were leaving today."

"Thought you wouldn't come in today."

"I couldn't stay home, I'd just sit there thinking about Clifford."

"I was really sorry to hear about that," Ellis began. "Especially after—"

Bevel interrupted. "It had nothing to do with you. Clifford would have been the same kind of dick to anyone who was in the bar last night. He was a real creep when he got stewed. Which was often. Still, he didn't deserve to die. Especially like he did. Jesus. The police told me about it."

"You shouldn't dwell on it."

"I know," she said. "Guess you really can't fault the bear, or wolf, or whatever it was. We humans keep encroaching on their territory. Can't expect every one of them to simply turn tail and run. Some are going to stay and fight, you know?"

"You're convinced it was an animal?"

"What else? Police said his body was ripped, torn, and chewed as well."

"So was my friend's," Ellis said, nodding toward the urn.

"Really? Well that just makes my point, right? Some damn rogue animal on the prowl."

"Maybe. Probably. Look, I'm going to stay until tomorrow. If you don't have to work too late, I'd like to take you to dinner or something. I meant what I told you before you left this morning. Last night was great. But with all that's happened… I thought you might not want to be alone tonight. No heavy breathing, you know. Just a couple of people having dinner together. Up to you."

"Yeah. Maybe dinner and a drink would be a good thing. I'm done at seven. Ted, the other bartender, has the late shift tonight. Tell you what, I'll make a reservation at Osteria for eight o'clock. It's just down the block on Federal Plaza. A five minute walk. Meet you there, okay?"

"Sounds great."

"Oh, you do like Italian, right?"

"Who doesn't," Ellis replied, standing, picking up his cremated friend, and walking away.

The restaurant took up one corner of a typical Santa Fe stucco building. It had a fenced-in patio for outdoor dining. Ellis hoped Bevel had asked for a spot there. The night was perfect for being under the stars. The host greeted him, took his name, checked the list, then showed him to a table in the corner of the patio. Luck was with him, he thought. Then he thought, yeah, bad luck. An old friend killed. Along with Bevel's ex. Jeez, he said to himself, *what the world throws at you from time to time.* Then he chided himself for bemoaning his situation when two men were dead long before they should have been. Sometimes just staying above ground is the luckiest thing of all, he mused. Ellis didn't have time to ruminate further. The host showed Bevel to the table. She was clad in a simple black dress with matching nails and deep purple lipstick.

"Hello," Ellis said rising. "You look lovely this evening."

"You don't clean up so bad yourself," she responded.

"Yeah, had my suit pressed. Took a shower. Everything."

"Like the look without the tie," she offered.

"Me too. But I've got a tie in my pocket. Just in case there was a dress code."

"Keep it there. You'll get less sauce on it that way."

"What? Have you seen me eat?"

"No. It's just that I know what the food is like here. Makes pigs of us all."

"Oink-oink. What would you like to drink?"

Aperitifs, a bottle of wine, and delicious Northern Italian cuisine managed to keep their conversation relatively benign until they could no longer disregard the obvious. He spoke of it first.

"There's no getting around fate, is there?"

"How so?"

"You know. You meet someone you like. Everything seems fine. Then the bottom falls out. You feel bad for... I don't know. You just feel like maybe if you hadn't..."

"Look," she cut in, "you have nothing to apologize for. A terrible thing happened to Clifford. But neither you or I had anything to do with that. I feel bad for him, but not for us.

"We met, enjoyed each other's company in more ways than one, and moved along. That's what you do in life. You just keep going. Whatever happens, happens. We don't really have much say in that regard."

"A fatalist, huh? Don't believe our lives are what we make them? Think we're all just being blown about by the winds of fate?"

"We have a lot of say, sure. But ultimately we don't have a lot of control. That's really an illusion. Try as we might, and succeed as often as we do, something always happens to make it obvious we may be calling our shots, but we're far from being in charge. We have to accept that," she said.

"I know what you mean," Ellis replied. "And your point is well taken. But for good or ill I'm one of those guys who's always looking for a way to be on top of things… to eliminate things that can go wrong… to keep mayhem to a minimum."

"And you're probably very good at it. But you're not perfect, are you?"

"Nobody is," he answered.

"That's my point," Bevel continued. "Imperfection will always raise its ugly head eventually. That doesn't have to change you, but the world becomes a much more tolerable place if you don't get bent out of shape every time things go to hell through no fault of your own."

"That's pretty insightful for a cocktail connoisseur."

"In my job, some degree of snappy repartee is frequently required."

"Not so much in mine. Thank heaven."

"Right," she intoned sarcastically. "I bet if you put your mind to it, you could debate existentialism 'til the cows come home."

"Can you think of anything less fun," he questioned.

"No," she immediately answered.

As they both chuckled, he raised his empty glass and said, "One more?"

"One is never enough and two now is too many," she said. "Perhaps we should call it a night."

Moments later Ellis was paying the check and offering to walk, drive, or see her home in whatever mode was appropriate. As good a time as they'd had, with all that had happened, he didn't feel right about asking her to join him in his room at the hotel. She didn't suggest it either. Sometimes negative incidents come between positive plans whether one wants them too or not.

She told Ellis that her car was just around the corner. He insisted on at least walking her there. As she was opening the door, he asked, "Are you working tomorrow?"

"I come on at noon," she said.

"I'll probably be gone by then, need to leave in the morning."

"Well, I guess this is it, then."

"You still have my card, right? It's got my phone and email on it."

"Yes, and you know where I work and how to get hold of me."

"If you're ever in San Diego—"

"Or the next time you're in Santa Fe."

"Oh, hell, Bevel."

"Just say good-bye and kiss me, Brig Ellis."

He did.

"CHECK SANCHEZ," ELLIS SAID.

Still on the ground like his squad mates, Fowler turned to the diminutive Sanchez to see if the spill they took made the knife wound worse. "You okay, bro?"

"Neck's stiffer. Can't turn my head much."

"Blood loss?" Ellis asked.

Tasso, who had moved up to check the wound himself, answered, "No worse."

Adams asked what the rest were wondering, "What now, Lieutenant?"

Hesitation in the face of chaos not only retards efficiency, it also implants doubt. And Ellis knew they were going to need all the confidence they could muster.

"Hump time. On your feet."

"Uh, Lieutenant," Devlin volunteered without being asked, "won't we run into whoever took out the bird?"

Fowler chimed in. "We'll likely be over-matched in men and muscle if they got shoulder-mounted firepower that can do what they did to that Blackhawk."

"That's why we're heading north," Ellis responded.

Wincing a bit before he spoke, Sanchez said, "But we came in from the South, right? That's the quickest way back to base camp... isn't it?"

"Listen," Ellis said—the tone of his voice conveying the gravity of his message—"we crossed the border coming in. We're in a country we're not supposed to be in. Going back the way we came will lead us into the middle of the force that took out the Blackhawk. We'll be outgunned, outmanned, and out of fucking options. We go north until we get to the mountains."

Fowler piped up. "That's a long-ass walk, Lieutenant,"

"One that just might keep you alive," Tasso interjected.

"Can the chatter. Switch positions," Ellis barked as he moved swiftly to take the point and Tasso circled to the rear. "Keep an eye on Sanchez," Ellis told Fowler. "Let's move."

CHAPTER 6

IT WAS STILL EARLY IN the morning, but Ordona and Wilcrest didn't knock. They had secured a master key from the young woman on duty at the hotel desk. Both men came through the door with guns drawn.

Seeing Ellis in the middle of packing, Ordona spoke as he holstered his weapon and took out a set of cuffs. "Hands behind your back, you're coming with us."

"What's going on? What is this?"

"You're under arrest."

"On what charge?"

"For the moment… murder."

"I thought we settled that. You checked my alibi with Bevel, right?"

"We did. And now your alibi's dead. That's the murder we're charging you with."

He heard it, but for a moment, he couldn't believe it. Bevel, dead? It couldn't be. She was so warm. So alive. What could have happened? As his hands were being cuffed behind his back, Ellis tried to find out.

"Ordona, what happened to her? And when? Please, tell me."

"We'll be asking the questions. And we'll do it at the station."

"But I was just about to check out?"

"Yeah, well, you're checking in with us now. Everything will be taken along. What's that," Ordona asked, pointing to the wood and brass urn on the desk.

"That's what I came to Santa Fe for. It's the remains of my friend, Vic Tasso."

"Wilcrest, take Mr. Tasso and this bag." Then turning back to Ellis, he said, "Where are your car keys?"

"They're in my right coat pocket. But I'm not in the habit of letting just anyone drive my car."

Ordona reached in Ellis's pocket, pulled out the keys, and tossed them to Wilcrest saying, "See that the car gets to the station as well."

"You're not going to take it apart, are you?"

"A proper search will be made. Whatever we take apart, we'll put back together."

"If anything's damaged," Ellis said, "I'll be particularly annoyed."

Ordona's reply was immediate. "Tell someone who gives a shit."

The ride to the station in the unmarked police sedan was quiet. Ellis assumed there was no way Ordona was going to share anything until the policeman was on his own turf and playing by his own rules. Even though he had been cuffed, he had not been read his Miranda rights. Ellis didn't think that was the kind of thing a detective like Ordona would simply forget. If he was really being arrested he could shut the whole show down immediately just by asking for a lawyer when they arrived at the station. *This is no bust*, Ellis said to himself. *They just want to grill me. Find out what I know. See if I'm going to lie about anything. Okay. I'll play. 'Cause I have a lot of things I want to find out too. Jesus. Bevel. Damn.*

The interrogation room had a table, three chairs, and the obligatory two-way mirror. Ellis was made to sit there alone for half an hour, which is difficult to do when you assume someone or more than just one someone is watching you from the other side of the glass. But he made a silent commitment to himself to keep his cool, realizing he'd be apt to learn a lot more being cooperative instead of combative. When Ordona finally opened the door and walked in, there was a woman with him. Ellis guessed her age at mid-thirties. She was tall and athletically thin. Her strawberry blonde hair was swept back in a French curl. Dressed in a white blouse and charcoal business suit, her coat did a less than complete job of covering the .32 police special on her hip. It didn't take Ellis long to assume that was probably intentional.

"I'm Carlyle," she said pulling out one of the chairs and sitting across from the P.I. while Ordona moved to one corner of the room and leaned against the wall. "I'd like to thank you for coming in today."

"Thank me? Well, it wasn't like I had much choice."

"Yes. There seems to have been some confusion about that. But I want to assure you that no charges have been filed at this time and this is merely an interview to see if you can be helpful in our investigation. We appreciate your willingness to help."

Ellis was a bit leery of her solicitous manner after Ordona's earlier tough-guy tactics. But most of all he wanted to know what happened to Bevel.

"Detective Ordona told me Bevel is dead."

"That's correct."

"Well, can you tell me about it?"

"We were hoping you could tell us."

"Look, I don't know anything about her death. Yes, we had

dinner together last night… but I assume you know that, or he wouldn't have rousted me, right?"

Carlyle was alarmingly straightforward. "We do know about your dinner. We had a tail on you last night."

"A tail? But I thought we resolved that yesterday morning. I couldn't have had anything to do with her ex-husband's death. She must have confirmed the fact that we were together night-before-last."

"She did. But there's always the chance that both of you planned his demise, executed that plan, and then provided an alibi for one another."

"But wait a minute," Ellis said. "I thought you guys were convinced some animal killed Clifford."

"We're definitely convinced of that," Carlyle responded. "We're just not sure if it's a hairy animal or a human animal."

"You're saying some person could be trying to make it look like an animal is responsible for the deaths."

"We're not saying anything at the moment. We're just exploring the possibilities. Plus the facts as we know them. And unfortunately, one of the facts is that you were involved with all three victims."

"Three?"

"The ex-Mrs. James, Mr. James, and Mr. Tasso."

"But I told Ordona I wasn't even in Santa Fe when Vic died."

"We're aware of what you said, Mr. Ellis, but we haven't established that conclusively yet. Until we do, we have only your word, which frankly we wouldn't accept outright from The Pope if he, like you, was the last person known to have seen Clifford and Bevel James alive."

"Please," Ellis began, "can we just get back to why I'm here right now? Exactly what happened to Bevel?"

Carlyle responded without benefit of notes. Ellis wondered

if she had one of those photographic memories. "The police received a call at approximately 3:15 this morning. The caller described hearing blood-curdling screams, violent thrashing about, and ungodly roars coming from the house next door. When a patrol car was dispatched to the scene, the officers found that the back screen door of the house had been ripped, torn, and yanked from its hinges. Entering, they found the body and immediately called in. We had an investigative team on the scene in less than an hour. The neighbor who made the initial call was brought over to provide an identification. After viewing the deceased, retching, plus almost fainting, the neighbor identified the victim as Bevel James. Once we leaned who the deceased was, we naturally sought the last person we were aware of who had seen her alive. That would be you. That's why you're here."

Ellis asked, "When did you say the call was made?"

"3:15."

"I was in the hotel, sound asleep at that time."

"Where were you an hour earlier?"

"Why do you ask?"

"Because that's when the neighbor said she heard all the noise."

"She waited an hour to call?"

"Thought she might have dreamed it at first. Tried to go back to sleep. Started feeling frightened, guilty, and eventually called in."

"So, if she had called when she heard something, Bevel might still be alive?"

"Hard to say," Carlyle answered. "Injuries were massive. Back to the question I just asked, where were you an hour earlier, at 2:15?"

"I was sound asleep, like I said. Came directly back to the

hotel from the restaurant and crashed about midnight."

"Can anyone verify that?"

"Of course no one can verify that, I was alone."

"Unlike the night before when the ex-Mrs. James joined you."

"Yes. Unlike the night before."

Carlyle was firing on all cylinders. She didn't let up. "Did you ask her? Did she turn you down? Did she tell you the sex wasn't really that great? Did that piss you off? Did you wait for a couple of hours, sneak out of the hotel, go to her place, and kill her?"

Ellis immediately answered her questions from back to front. "No, I didn't kill her. I don't even know where she lives. I never sneaked out of the hotel. I wasn't angry. Anything she said about the night before is none of your business. She didn't turn me down because I didn't ask her to join me."

"So, the sex wasn't that great, huh? Or you would have asked for an encore."

This time, Ellis decided an annoyed expression and no answer would be his answer.

"Okay, so you're a gentleman, you don't want to talk about it. Understood. It's just that we don't get many private investigators that are gentlemen, so you can understand our reluctance to swallow your protestations whole."

"What?"

"That's w-h-o-l-e, whole, not h-o-l-e, hole."

Ellis grinned. "Carlyle, you are a piece of work. Does this interrogation technique of yours actually work?"

"Only on lesser intellects."

"So you assumed I would fall into that category."

"Saw your occupation, made that assumption. Snafu on my part."

"Well, we all make assumptions," Ellis said. "Want to hear some of mine?"

"I'm on the edge of my chair."

"Okay, you must be Captain, or at the least Lieutenant Carlyle because you made a point not to mention your rank when you introduced yourself. I figure that's less about modesty and more about not wanting to embarrass Ordona over there, because he's older but has to work underneath you. No pun intended. You made me wait a half hour to put me on edge. At this point you probably think it's unlikely, but still possible I might have something to do with the killings. By hassling me, you're buying time while your team takes my car apart looking for potential weapons that could be used to kill with animal-like ferocity. I want you to know, I'm very partial to that car and will not take it lightly if it sustains any damage."

"Ordona mentioned that. I bet him you'd mention it again. I won." Looking over at the detective still leaning against the wall, Carlyle said, "So… coffees, please. Three. I assume you want one, Mr. Ellis."

"There you go with those assumptions again. But you're right this time. Black. No sugar."

"Same," Carlyle said, followed by Ordona silently removing himself and his pained expression from the wall, opening the door, and exiting.

"It's Lieutenant Carlyle by the way. Special Crimes Division. And he doesn't work under me, but he doesn't work over me either. That's what makes my division special. And that's why I like it."

"Careful," Ellis said, "I sense your professionally distant demeanor cracking a bit."

"I'm simply relaxing my artificially intimidating modus operandi because Ordona's not in the room now. That, and I know a bit about you that I haven't shared with my compatriots yet."

"Which would be?"

"You have an especially curious personnel record. Seems it's heavily redacted as far as assignments and operations go. While it lists your qualifications and accomplishments like officer candidate school, ranger training, airborne, and the rest, it's exceedingly oblique about time in grade and duty stations. While participation is noted in major operations in Iraq, Saudi, Syria and more, there's very little about what you actually did from place to place or country to country. I believe Colombia and Venezuela were mentioned too, but actual activity there seems to be clandestine as well."

"So, you have a pipeline to military records and you got a bit of background on me. Exactly how does that make you more willing to believe what I have to say."

"By itself, it doesn't really, but when I followed it up by checking with individuals in the San Diego Police Department who have knowledge of the P. I.s in your city, I kept hearing comments like straight-shooter, good-guy, wish-they-were-all-like-him. Made me a bit nauseous to tell you the truth, but at least it was better than window-peeper, insurance scammer, and sleazeball, which I usually get when I look into private eyes."

"And when did you do all this," Ellis asked.

"When your name came up day before yesterday."

"Resourceful, aren't you?"

"Just thorough, and a bit anal retentive. Ordona and the guys hate that about me."

"Yet what you learned is apparently still not enough to keep you from grilling me and giving my car the once-over."

"I take everything with that proverbial grain of salt, Ellis.

But as long as your car gets a clean bill of health, then I'm willing to explore options we've touched on."

"Such as," Ellis said.

"Such as, one, there really is some wild-ass animal running amok and killing people. Two, some person, or persons, is trying to make it *look* like a wild-ass animal is running amok and killing people. Three, some person, or persons, has some type of badass bobcat on a leash, or whatever, and is letting it loose on people."

"Aside from your vivid descriptions, is there a common denominator among those options?"

"Try to keep up, Ellis. It's the one I mentioned before. All the victims, in one way or another, were connected to you."

Before Ellis had a chance to respond, Ordona opened the door with one hand and used his other to set down the tray holding three cups of coffee. He turned to Carlyle and said, "Car came out clean. Nothing hidden."

The Special Crimes Division Lieutenant looked at the three coffees which appeared identical. She asked Ordona, "These all the same?"

He couldn't help but grin. "Don't they look the same?"

"They'd all look the same," she pointed out, "even if there were sugar or sweetener in one or more of them."

Had there been a light bulb in the room, it would have glowed over Ordona's head. "Oh yeah, guess they would, wouldn't they?"

Carlyle managed to keep her eyes from rolling. Then she passed one of the coffees to Ellis. She moved one Ordona's way and took the last one for herself.

"So, here's the thing," Carlyle began. "There's obviously a connection between the three killings other than they look animal induced. Tasso and the first James could be a coincidence, but Mr. James followed by ex-Mrs. James is simply too close for coincidence and too non-random to be one of nature's creatures with a taste for human flesh. If we nail down, which I assume we will, the fact that you were not in Santa Fe when Tasso was killed, that blows a hole in you being directly responsible for all three."

Ellis didn't miss the qualifier, "Directly?"

"Hey, just because you may not have been here doesn't totally clear you of having something to do with it. Ever hear of murder for hire? It's almost a cottage industry these days."

"And just how much does a bear or a cougar get for a hit," Ellis quipped.

"Not very funny, but clever enough to break my train of thought."

"You were indicating that I'm probably not directly responsible for three killings."

"Right," Carlyle snapped, then re-engaged. "So, let's take it a step further, let's say A, it's not animal-only killings, and B, you're not the killer, the buyer of the kills, or a psycho lion tamer with a mountain cat on a leash. That leads to C, someone wants to make it look like you're the killer."

"Interesting supposition."

"It is. Isn't it? Of course, as yet, there's a rather gaping hole in the middle of it. A hole you could fill in for Detective Ordona and me."

Ellis responded with one word. "Motive?"

"Bingo," Carlyle said. "Why would someone want to make it appear that you're involved not only with murder, but with such gruesome, predator-like kills?"

"Unfortunately, I don't have the slightest idea," Ellis said.

"You may not now, but I bet with more thought, something will come to you."

"Hey, wait a minute. You're not going to keep me here until I come up with some possible motive are you?"

"No. Since you, your hotel room, and your car seem to be clean, we're going to let you go on to Sedona to fulfill your promise to Mr. Tasso."

"And if something comes to me," Ellis began, "I'll just call or email, right?"

"Wrong," Carlyle answered. "You can just tell me. Because I'll be going with you."

THEY HUSTLED OVER THE SAME ground they'd covered initially, but the pace was swifter. The predators had become the prey and they were in a big hurry to put distance between themselves and whoever was on their tail.

At a small but natural break in the foliage, Ellis gave a hand signal for everyone to stop. It was passed down the line. When all were kneeling, he went back quickly to check on Sanchez.

"How you doing, soldier?"

"Neck's really stiff now, Lieutenant. Can't turn my head. But I can keep going."

"Okay. Soon as we get to the compound where we took out the hostiles we'll grab some food and water to take with us and have a look at your wound. It's just a couple more klicks."

"Good to go, Sir."

They picked up the pace, pushing aside anything that impeded their momentum. Soon, they reached the edge of the wood and held momentarily before crossing the clearing to the house.

Ellis gave instructions. "Once we're over the retaining wall, Adams... you, Devlin, and Fowler, pick up whatever water and food you can carry. It's going to need to last us. Tasso and I will have a look at Sanchez and see if we need to do anything before moving on. Remember, anything you can carry that we can eat or drink and—"

One, two, three massive explosions hit sequentially. The house, the wall, the bodies that were still inside and out, blew into the night sky and rained down in flaming pieces. The squad burrowed into the ground like armadillos and hoped the cascading debris wouldn't land on top of them. As the smoke cleared enough to see what had transpired, Ellis looked wide-eyed at what was now nothing but level ground and charred remnants. The entire compound had been flattened. There was nothing to secure. Nothing to take with them. And no time to bitch about it.

"Everybody up. Let's go. *Now!*"

CHAPTER 7

THE SIX HOUR DRIVE FROM Santa Fe, New Mexico, to Sedona, Arizona, turned out to be as interesting inside the car as outside. While, admittedly, it was difficult to compete with the western landscape and its natural beauty, Carlyle's long, tanned legs in hiking shorts definitely gave the spectacular scenery a run for its money. She had dressed down for comfort and Ellis was the beneficiary. Of course, it was somewhat more difficult for him to keep his eyes on the road and his mind on their shared desire to figure out why someone would want to make him look like a crazed killer. While Carlyle's attire didn't help, her conversation did as she kept mining for more information—information that Ellis only gave out sparingly after running his own mental traps before answering, because nothing was making sense to him. Not how or why Tasso was killed, and certainly not why someone was trying to make it look like he was involved. Maybe he had to take his thinking beyond the specifics, past Tasso and Bevel and her ex-husband. But he'd have to do it while dealing with Carlyle's relentless pursuit of motive and more.

She had been as upfront as a cop was likely to be with a suspect, even one as tangential as Ellis. She had said her reason for tagging along was to continue to probe, and he believed that. But he wondered if she had another reason as well. Did she think Ellis was in danger too—in danger of perhaps being the next victim, himself? That would be a tight way to wrap it up, he mused. Make it look like the killer has ended it all by killing himself. But again the question kept coming back to why? Why was any of it happening?

Carlyle interrupted his contemplation. "You haven't said much for the last thirty miles or so."

"Just thinking," Ellis replied.

"Sometimes thinking gets in the way of thinking."

"That sounds sophomorically profound. What's it supposed to mean?"

"It means that sometimes the best way to figure something out, is to stop trying to figure it out and let your conscious mind wander into other areas. That way, your unconscious mind is liberated and can free-associate… often popping out an answer to some problem you've been fixated on but unable to solve."

"And that's a bona fide criminal justice technique, is it?"

"Not really, just something that works for me every now and then."

"Okay," Ellis began, "let's forget about a potential killer's theoretical motive for now and talk about something else. Like your motive for being here."

"I told you before. In addition to helping you think things through, and being able to keep an eye on you, I'm pretty compulsive when it comes to people killing other people in my own backyard. If I have to go outside my yard to get them, I'm more than happy to do so."

"Relentless type, are you?"

"I've been described that way," Carlyle said.

"By your cohorts… like Ordona?"

"Yep. And others. What about you? How do people describe you?"

"You said you got playback on me when you talked to the San Diego P. D."

"That's true. But what about people who put you on the liability, rather than the asset side of the ledger?"

Ellis thought for a moment before he spoke. "They'd probably say stubborn, opinionated, too old school for a new age world. That sort of thing."

"A traditionalist, huh? How so?"

"I prefer Sinatra to Adele… read books on paper instead of screens… can't stand video games, reality TV, or movies made from comic books."

"That sounds less like a traditionalist and more like a reactionary."

"Not a big fan of labels, either. Too easy to categorize before you really take the time to know someone."

"How well did you know Victor Tasso?" Carlyle asked.

"Pretty well, I think. At least during the time we spent together."

"And that was all in the service?"

"Yeah. You talk about keeping up with one another once you get out… but it seldom happens."

"Why did he ask you, specifically, to do what you're doing for him?"

"We were warriors. Went through some hairy times together. Had to depend on each other more than once. Surprised me when he asked if I'd be the one to spread his ashes should the time come. But that's not really the kind of thing you can say no to."

"He must have thought pretty highly of you. Or he wouldn't have asked."

"Hard to tell what some people think. Particularly an Apache. Like to keep their own counsel."

"Still, he asked and you not only said yes, you actually committed to it. Must have been some kind of bond there. Were you that close with other soldiers in your outfit?"

"Close. But not as close. Part of being an officer, a leader in the military, is keeping your distance."

"You didn't want guys to like you?" She asked.

"Being liked is okay. Being respected is better. People who respect you will follow orders faster, and they'll be more likely to take on challenges they may initially think they can't overcome."

"Have many of those challenges?"

"Quite a few."

"Guess you overcame them all or you wouldn't be here."

"Some you overcome. Some you just manage to get through," Ellis said, stealing a glance in his rear view mirror.

"Notice you've been doing that a lot."

"What?"

"Looking to see what's behind you. Think someone's tailing you," Carlyle answered.

"Don't you? Isn't that one of the reasons you wanted to come along? Let's face it. Whoever's doing this can't make it look like I'm doing it if he's not where I am."

"That's true. But he doesn't necessarily have to follow you to do that."

"What do you mean?"

"Maybe he knows where you're going before you get there."

"Psychic, is he?"

"Doesn't have to be," Carlyle began. "Maybe somehow he knew about the commitment you had to Tasso. So he just had to wait for you to come to Santa Fe. Maybe he knows you're going to Sedona. Maybe he left before you did and he's there already… waiting for you."

"That's a lot of maybes."

"Got one more. Maybe it was just his good luck that you came to Santa Fe. And he took advantage of your presence to make it look like you did it. Then did the other two as insurance and to make you look even worse."

"You don't believe that. Or you wouldn't have come along."

"True, I don't put much stock in lucking into anything. But you have to consider every possibility, or you might miss something."

"I can do that."

"Can you? Then why do you keep referring to the perp as a he? Could be a she, you know. Or even an it. Still can't completely rule out an animal."

"Oh… now I see," Ellis said.

"See what?"

"Now I see why you're often described as relentless."

Approaching Sedona, it became obvious why it was once named the most beautiful town in America. Spectacular mountains and cliffs rose from the earth in colors of salmon and cream. Gigantic vistas stretched above meandering canyons that seemed to go on forever. On the outskirts of the city, the fantastic formations of Bell, Coffeepot, and Cathedral Rock, were testament to divinely inspired sculpture or nature's unfathomable handiwork, depending on your particular belief system. What was undeniable was the awe-inspiring grandeur of the natural world that surrounded eclectic homes of the wealthy, modest houses of the working class, and makeshift dwellings of the poverty-stricken. Beauty was available for all. The degree to which it could be enjoyed was like most things in life, dependent upon what one was willing or able to pay.

Ellis had made his reservation at the Hilton prior to beginning his trip, so Carlyle had booked a room there as well. After checking in, they each retired for a shower and perhaps a quick nap before dinner. The next day they would drive to the Yavapai Apache Reservation to fulfill Ellis's promise to Tasso.

Carlyle decided on a bath rather than a shower. She filled the tub with hot water and added the Aveda soaking salts that had previously been stored in her overnight bag. Destressing was definitely in order. Though she'd never admit it to Ellis, the long ride and even longer intellectual hunt for motive and murderer had worn her out. Submerging herself in billowy bubbles was the perfect antidote for her cerebral system overload. Turning off the taps, it didn't take long for her to drift into a kind of half sleep with only her head above the silent stillness that surrounded her.

Ellis let the cascading water from the shower pulsate over his taught muscles made even tighter from the six-hour drive. He was fatigued in mind as well as body and eager to put his continuing questions on hold. As the spray bounced off his face and ran in rivulets down his trunk, arms, and legs, he thought about the recuperative power of water, and how almost everyone takes it for granted. Water, it seems to always be around, always easily accessible. Except of course, when it isn't, often when it's vital. It was the water that took what Carlyle had referred to as Ellis's unconscious mind back in time. Back to when he and Tasso and others needed water and didn't have it.

"**F**ORGET SUPPLIES. THEY'RE ASHES NOW. Got to keep moving," Ellis told Tasso.

"But if we're going the long way..."

"That's our only way. Staying here we become nothing but targets. Going back we're either dead or prisoners. Dead would be preferable."

Tasso responded, "You know what we'll have to cross... if we even get that far."

"I know. But that's where we're going. Take the point."

Tasso moved to the head of the column, Ellis made his way to the back. As he passed Fowler, he asked about Sanchez. "How's he doing?"

"Still on his feet with that damn knife sticking out the back of his neck. One tough little dude, ain't he?"

"Let's hope he can keep it up. Let me know if anything changes."

Nothing did for the next few hours. The squad kept moving north as the night threatened to end with the first pink light of dawn, quickly followed by the first signs that even bad times can get worse. Sanchez's gait became erratic. As he walked, he would keep his head straight but he would sway to one side. First to the left, then back to the right, as if he were careening like a drunk on shipboard from one side of the deck to the next. Fowler became concerned. He turned and signaled to Ellis who jogged up from the rear.

"He's getting wobbly, Lieutenant. Afraid he might fall."

Tasso, still on point, heard the voices behind him and motioned for Devlin and Adams to halt.

"Let's take five," Ellis said. "Fowler, help me get Sanchez over there. We'll get him off his feet and lean his back against that boulder."

As the two were seating the injured man, Tasso circled back to them and asked without asking, "Sanchez?"

"Yeah," Ellis said. "I think that blade needs to come out."

Tasso reminded him, "If it starts to bleed, Lieutenant, there's no gauze or bandages to wrap it with… and no water to clean the wound."

"Well, for now, we can deal with half of that," Ellis said pulling his shirt tail out and beginning to unbutton it. "We'll cut strips of my undershirt for gauze. Use pieces from the tunic for bandages if we need them." In less than a minute Ellis was naked from the waist up. With his knife, he cut the undershirt he had been wearing into something resembling squares. Then he sliced the long sleeves from his tunic and cut them into manageable strips. "Won't be very sanitary," Ellis said, but it will have to do." Then giving the cut cloth to Tasso, he motioned for the Apache to move behind the injured man.

"You still with us, Sanchez," Ellis asked.

"Must be. We're talking to each other, right Lieutenant?"

"In just a second we're going to get that damn blade out of your neck."

"Probably gonna hurt, ain't it?" the Mexican asked.

Ellis gave a nod and in one swift, fluid move, Tasso grasped the handle and pulled the knife free—

"Fuuuuuuck!" Sanchez screamed.

"Bleeding, Sergeant?"

"Affirmative."

"Apply pressure." Then turning to Fowler, Ellis said, "Help Tasso. Pad it, then wrap it tight. Sanchez. Look at me. Sanchez, how are you feeling?"

"Little woozy, sir."

"You're pretty hard core, Corporal."

"Been stabbed before. I'm from the barrio."

"How you guys coming?" Ellis asked.

"Bandaged," Tasso responded. "Let's give Sanchez another minute or two," Ellis said.

"Then what?" Fowler asked.

"Then we hump the hell out of here."

CHAPTER 8

ELLIS HAD ASKED CARLYLE IF she wanted to join him for dinner. She asked him if anything had popped into his head about possible motives. When he said no, she said no, advising that she'd opt for room service followed by early lights out. Ellis was actually relieved. Even though Carlyle was an attractive woman, her constant questions weren't. He was happy for the time alone to let his own mind wander. Still, not being fond of eating in his room, he went down to the restaurant in the hotel to treat himself to a steak and a couple of glasses of Cabernet.

It was definitely out of the ordinary for Ellis to spend a lot of time thinking about his military days, but that's what he did as he consumed his meal and his wine. He had done a good job of putting both good and bad memories behind him when he mustered out. Of course, getting word about Tasso's death brought a lot of it back. And the subsequent events following the Apache's demise kept Ellis's thoughts returning to the days they spent together in and out of danger's grasp. Was there a key there? A key to unlock why these brutal murders were going on and why someone was trying to paint a portrait of him as the killer. He felt there must be, though he didn't feel right about sharing all his thoughts with Carlyle just yet. Ellis wanted to find out a few things for himself first—potentially important things—but things that could wait until he fulfilled his promise to Tasso.

The following morning, after getting together for breakfast, Ellis and Carlyle drove to the Yavapai Apache Nation Reservation. Assuming they were going to spend some time off of what most considered beaten paths, they had both dressed accordingly; loose fitting shirts, shorts, and hiking boots. In the car, they followed the signs and pulled up in front of the Administration Building. As Ellis was turning the engine off, Carlyle asked, "You going to take him in with you?"

"Who?"

"You're friend, Tasso."

"Think we should get our bearings first."

"Good. You are going to tell them what you plan to do here, right?"

"Yes. Why wouldn't I?"

"Well, some people wouldn't, you know. They'd just try to swing in, do their thing, and be on their way before anyone was the wiser. Some people are like that."

"Well, I'm not," Ellis replied. "I plan to explain the situation and get any help I can."

"A man after my own heart. Not too macho to ask for assistance. Mind if I join you?"

"You've come this far. Might as well go all the way."

"Okay, but once we actually get wherever we're supposed to be, if you want some privacy, just let me know. I don't want to butt in where I'm not needed or wanted."

"That's very kind of you. For now, let's just see what's involved."

Thirty minutes later, having spoken with William Three-Feathers, The Reservation Administrative Executive, Ellis and Carlyle were walking back to the car. The man had been more than helpful. He informed the pair that he had known some of the Tasso family long ago, but that Victor had been the last of the line. He was also willing to give them some insight about the best place to spread the Apache's ashes, even adding a hand-drawn addendum of a private spot off a public hiking trail where they wouldn't be bothered by tourists and other visitors to the reservation.

"A real gentleman," Carlyle said. "Very kind of him to help."

"Yeah. Of course, your badge and credentials didn't hurt. But he did go out of his way to do more than was asked of him. Kind of reminded me of Vic that way."

They got in the car and drove to the parking area for the different hiking trails. Ellis opened the trunk and took out the urn. He placed it in a backpack that he then slipped over his shoulders. Looking for all the world like just another couple out for a walk in the now civilized wilderness, the two started down the well-worn path the administrator had suggested.

As they passed beneath the fabled red rocks that surrounded them and among the sun-burned tourists beside them, they kept an eye out for the cutoff William Three-Feathers had marked on their trail guide. Eventually spotting what they presumed was it, they waited until no one was nearby. Then slowly and cautiously they started up what initially appeared to be a rock-strewn goat path that meandered through scrub bushes, past ocatillo cactus, and under pinion and oak trees. Ascending the grade was arduous, but when the difficult route eventually opened onto a crested butte, complaints regarding physical challenges were quickly put behind them.

The view was magnificent. A one-hundred and eighty degree panorama spread out before them—the lush Verde Valley on one side, and on the other, the outline of Montezuma Wells—according to legend, birthplace of the Yavapai people. Both

Ellis and Carlyle stood in wonder for a moment, realizing there could be no better place than this to return Victor Tasso to the land of his ancestors.

Ellis took the backpack off and pulled the urn out. "I'm going near the cliff's edge," he told Carlyle.

"Okay. I'll just stay back here. Never have been crazy about heights."

Ellis nodded and walked toward the rim. Once there, he dropped to one knee and opened the vessel that held the last remnants of his friend and fellow warrior. He paused momentarily, wondering first if he should say something, then wondering what it might be. What can you say about the end of life as we know it? *Some things truly are beyond understanding,* Ellis told himself as he began to remove the lid.

Behind him, Carlyle watched in silence, the situation providing a sense of solemnity even though she had never known the deceased. Then suddenly, she felt a shock at the base of her skull, just below her left ear. It was a piercing pain like the sting of an enraged wasp. Her hand involuntarily moved toward her head as if to ward off further assault, but before it could get there her eyes rolled back, her knees buckled, and she crumpled to the ground.

The whir of the wind and the weight of Ellis's thoughts masked Carlyle's fall behind him. Looking out at the remarkable vista, he rose and slowly turned the urn over. The breeze then whisked its contents into the sky and across the majestic wilderness that had surrounded everything in it for thousands of years. "Good-bye, Vic," he said. "We did what we had to."

Only a few seconds had elapsed since Carlyle went down. When Ellis turned, he saw the fallen Lieutenant, then rushed to her. Those few seconds were all that it took to reload the

Pneu-Dart G2 X-Caliber rifle and fire a second projectile. This time toward Ellis. The needle struck him in the side of his neck. Like Carlyle, he instinctively reached for the pain. He managed to grab the elongated cylinder and pull it out, but not before it had released its load of carfentanil into his bloodstream. As he struggled to keep his wits about him and to see if Carlyle was still breathing, Ellis's head became heavy. It rolled back on his shoulders. He looked up into the glare of the blazing sun and wondered for just a moment why it and everything around him was turning black.

THEY HAD SLOWED THEIR PACE. A necessity for Sanchez. While it ran the risk of shortening the distance between the squad and their pursuers, Ellis counted on the fact that his tiny band could cover ground more swiftly than the larger force trailing them. He also knew if the squad could reach the destination he had in mind, the enemy would not follow.

The makeshift bandages that had wrapped Sanchez's wound seemed to be holding. While the bleeding hadn't stopped entirely, it had slowed dramatically. Ellis knew he'd have to stop and change the dressings as often as he could if bleeding was to be kept to a minimum. The Mexican Corporal was gamely holding his own though. Frequently staggering and occasionally stumbling, he managed to keep moving forward as the men directly behind him kept vigil. Ellis would let him go as far as he could for as long as he could before revising tactics that might compromise their escape.

Beneath the cover of dense foliage, as the sun was reaching its zenith, Tasso circled back and spoke to Ellis. "We're getting close. You're sure you want to do this."

"I'm sure I don't want to do it. But it's our only shot now."

"They may balk," the Apache said, referencing the other squad members.

Ellis responded. "If you and I don't, they won't."

Tasso nodded and returned to take point.

Fifteen minutes later, they reached the end of the growth that had surrounded them. Their vertical formation turned into a horizontal one as each man walked up, stood beside the other, and gazed out at what was before them.

Ellis knew what they were thinking. So he lost no time in addressing it.

"It's called La Malplena Kvarano... The Empty Quarter. And it's as barren as it looks. Nothing grows. Nothing lives. No trees shade the way. No water. Nothing to eat. But on the other side... the border... allies... safety."

Devlin spoke first. "How far across, Lieutenant?"

Tasso answered for him. "What difference does it make?"

"Need somethin' to shoot for," Fowler volunteered.

"Less than ten," Ellis said.

"Klicks?" Adams asked.

"Days." Ellis answered.

"Motherfuck!" Fowler boomed. "Ten days with no food or water? Are you nuts?"

Tasso spoke. "Less than ten, the Lieutenant said. And less means less."

Ellis felt he owed them the truth, with a bit of motivation thrown in. "Believe it or not, we have the advantage, gentlemen. The hostiles on our tail won't follow us across."

"Yeah. That's because they're not fuckin' insane," Fowler said.

"But if there's no cover, what about planes, drones, whatever," Devlin asked.

"It's a no-fly zone that both sides are respecting so far. Look, like I said before. They have a vastly superior force. We make a stand here, we go down fighting, but we definitely go down.

We let them take us prisoner… your friends and family get to see you being beheaded on television and the Internet. We go for it… we at least give ourselves a chance."

"We going to take some kind of vote or something?" Adams asked.

"No," Tasso interjected.

"In case you ladies forgot," Ellis said, "you're not politicians, you're soldiers. This little discussion was a smoke break, and break's over."

Silence prevailed only a second before Sanchez stepped forward and said, "Come on you pussies, last one across buys the first round."

CHAPTER 9

THE BOTTOM OF A WELL. Hearing pieces of sounds he couldn't distinguish. Seeing shadows and shades of black he couldn't quite bring into focus. An odd sensation of floating—floating slowly toward the surface. A surface that hovered somewhere above him and beckoned him to rise. Heavy, heavy eyelids. So heavy he didn't think he could lift them. Until he did.

Snow blindness. A white, piercing light he not only saw but felt in his temples. Sounds. The wind. The rustle of leaves. Smells. The crispness of air in his nostrils. Arms and legs he wanted to move, but they seemed so heavy and confined. Then, like awakening from a dream, focus and memory returned. He had been on the butte overlooking the vista, but he wasn't there now. As he looked around, he realized why his limbs felt so constrained. He was literally wedged up against a boulder and covered over with broken tree limbs and scrub grass. Not buried, just hidden, it seemed.

He stretched his arms and legs to push himself free, shoving the improvised camouflage away. Feeling a pain in his neck as he moved, he reached up and touched where the projectile had entered. It was swollen and sore, but it was quickly put out of his mind as he simultaneously tried to get his bearings and look for Carlyle. Haphazardly pushing rocks and brush aside, he twisted and snaked his way from where he had been initially to any place that looked remotely similar to where they had been. Luck moved him in the right direction and eventually he found himself emerging from a wooded downslope and back onto the path that led to the butte. He wasn't sure he wanted to—afraid of what he might find—but he scrambled over to the cliff's edge anyway and looked below. Pristine as before. No mangled body to mar its beauty that Ellis could see. As he looked around, he also realized what he *didn't* see. No backpack or open urn lying where he had left them. But there was no time to concern himself about that. He was now singularly focused on finding Carlyle. So he stepped away from the cliff's edge and began to root through the surrounding underbrush calling her name, "Carlyle… Carlyle… Carlyle!" to no avail.

Ellis looked for signs of tracks, or footprints, or drag marks that might indicate where she had gone, or more ominously, where she might have been taken. But the ground was too rocky and dry to provide information. He wasn't sure how long he'd been unconscious, but he quickly realized it was now twilight and soon it might prove too dark to get back to the hiking trail they had taken initially. Ellis made the decision to retrace his steps, as best as he could remember them, get back to civilization, and secure help in finding Carlyle.

By the time he re-emerged from the secluded path, darkness had fallen and the hiking trail was long empty. He followed it back to the parking area where his car was the lone occupant. Jumping in and starting it, he raced back to the Administration Building where he hoped to find help. A pickup truck was in the lot and a light was still on so Ellis parked and ran inside.

Upon seeing the P.I. dash into his office, William Three-Feathers exclaimed, "It's you! Are you all right?"

"I'm okay," Ellis responded breathlessly. "I need help finding Lieutenant Carlyle."

"She's already been found."

"What? Is she okay? Has she been hurt?"

"She's alive… or at least, she was when they medivacked her out."

"What happened?" Ellis asked. Then immediately ordered. "Tell me."

"You don't know. You didn't see the attack?"

"What attack? Look, be specific. What happened and where is she?"

"She was terribly mauled. An animal. Bear or cougar, perhaps. Hard to tell initially. Luckily, hikers found her and we were able to get a chopper over for a LifeFlight to Phoenix. The Banner-University Medical Center."

"But that's hours away. Sedona's just—"

"It's not hours by helicopter. And Sedona doesn't have the trauma center help she was in need of. But what happened to you? Where have you been? People were looking for you."

"People?"

"Volunteers. Hikers who were on the reservation already. And the authorities. We were afraid you might have suffered a fate worse than hers… though that would be almost impossible."

"What's the drive time to Phoenix from here?"

"Couple of hours more or less. But look, you've got cuts and scratches all over you. Let's take you to the reservation clinic. They can clean you up and—"

"No time. I'm okay anyway."

"Well, I'll call the police and let them know you're alive and to some degree well. I'm sure they'll want to ask you some questions."

Ellis didn't want to take time to explain. But he did want

to continue the deception he had already initiated. "Look, Do me a favor. I'm on my way to that hospital in Phoenix. I need to make sure she's okay. I can answer any questions after I've seen her."

"But I really should let them know. They're probably setting up a search now, to look for you tomorrow."

"Let them know a search isn't necessary. That's fine. Tell them I'll answer any questions they have in Phoenix, after I've seen her. Just do that for me, okay."

"I'll tell them… but are you sure you're okay to drive?"

"I'm sure. Thanks."

Ellis dashed out as quickly as he had bolted in. By the time he was in his car and turning on the engine, William Three-Feathers was on the phone explaining to the authorities that Ellis had been found, was alive, and about two hours from now, could be found at the Banner University Medical Center in Phoenix. The first two things he told them were facts. Three-Feathers didn't realize that the third was fiction.

DRY, CRACKED EARTH. AS FAR as the eye could see. A tapestry of concentric lines forming squares, octagons, and trapezoidal shapes creating a floor of hell without the flames. This was what they walked into as they began their trek.

Sanchez, who had initially taken the lead, had fallen back to his accustomed place in the middle of the column. It wasn't necessary to walk single file, but it was easier for the men to keep their eyes on one another this way, and with Ellis at the rear, it was an effective way of making sure the column didn't stretch too far between bodies. Staying part of the group was vital. Drifting too far back or to the side, could lead to separation. Separation could lead to accidental abandonment.

They had gone two days without food or drink. No one mentioned it. As if stating the obvious would make things even worse. Thinking or talking about it wouldn't help. There was only one recourse. Cross the empty quarter before strength and will gave out. The latter perhaps even more important than the former.

On the far, flat horizon the sun was beginning to set. Ellis called for the men to stop.

He gathered them round so he wouldn't have to raise his voice.

"The sun's going down but we're not. Starting now, we'll walk by night and rest during the day. It will be cooler and we should be able to make better time. But I don't want to waste this night. So we'll keep going north."

"How do we keep from getting lost, Lieutenant, and walking around in circles," Adams asked.

"We'll navigate the way sea captains used to do it, by the stars. Should actually be more accurate than trying to keep on track in daylight."

Devlin piped up, "What's the matter, sir, compass on your watch not field functional?"

"Afraid I banged it on Fowler's head the last time he asked a stupid question," Ellis joked. "Only working intermittently. Kind of like Adams over there. But no matter. We've got a bona fide star reader in Sergeant Tasso."

"Yeah," Fowler interjected, "he'll keep us on the mystic but enlightened path. Won't you, Geronimo."

"I'll keep a boot up your ass if you don't move out," Tasso replied. "This way."

There was some chuckling as the squad moved out. There would be none of it in the days ahead.

CHAPTER 10

ELLIS'S MIND WAS RACING AS hard as his car's engine, which was humming smoothly down the highway but not toward Phoenix. Telling Three-Feathers that's where he was going was simply a ruse to buy him more time. He was actually heading back to the Hilton in Sedona with three steps in mind. He would call the hospital in Phoenix to check on Carlyle. He would clean up and check out as soon as he could. He would somehow manage to vanish from the grid for a while. All three were important for different reasons.

As soon as the Santa Fe police learned of Carlyle's attack, Ordona would immediately assume Ellis had something to do with it. He had no doubt the detective would contact Arizona authorities and an all-points-bulletin would be put out on him. Ellis knew he couldn't help himself or anyone else if he was behind bars. Hopefully, the police and highway patrol would believe what he told Three-Feathers, take the bait, and look for him on the way to or in Phoenix. Certainly if Carlyle survived, she would tell the authorities he was not involved. But he didn't know if she'd make it. Pulling his cell phone out of his pocket as he drove, he looked at it, then changed his mind and decided to wait until he reached the hotel to check on her. He didn't want to stop and the last thing he needed was a traffic mishap.

Arriving at the hotel, he went straight to his room thinking about how to make the call. If he used the phone in his room, there would be a record of it and the police would know he doubled back to Sedona. He pulled out his smart phone, looked up the Phoenix hospital number and punched it in. As he listened to it ring, it occurred to him that using his phone after this would enable the authorities to track him. He'd definitely need to pick up a burner.

"Banner University Medical Center. How may I direct your call?"

"A police Lieutenant was brought in earlier," Ellis began, "a trauma patient via LifeFlight. The name is Carlyle. I need to check on her condition."

"Carlyle? And what would be her first name?"

It occurred to Ellis he had no idea. "I'm… I don't know… I mean, she's a Santa Fe police Lieutenant who was helicoptered in. How many of those can you possibly have?"

"Sir, I'm not made aware of how our patients arrive."

"Can you just check, please? Or connect me to the trauma center or emergency room, maybe they'll know."

"Well, look at this. It seems we have only one Carlyle at the moment. The patient's in the ICU ward. I'll connect you."

As he waited, Ellis looked in the mirror and got a look at his frightful state. Dirt all over. Scratches on his arms, legs, and head. *God, I need a shower,* he thought to himself. *But not a shave. If I'm going to disappear for a while I should look as different as I can.*

"Intensive Care Unit. Nurse Meyers speaking."

"Nurse Meyers. You have a trauma patient there. Her name's Carlyle. I need to know how she is."

"I'm sorry. We're not allowed to provide information over the phone."

"Please, Nurse Meyers… she's my sister, I'm calling all the way from Buffalo, New York. I need to know how she's doing." While the content was a lie, the concern was real. And long, lonely night vigils sometimes have a way of overriding unsympathetic protocols. Especially for talkative nurses.

"Well, since you're calling from so far away. She's stable at the moment, but definitely in serious condition. The doctors said it may be some time before they can be certain she'll pull through."

"Jesus!"

"But your sister's a fighter, sir. That much is certain. With the injuries she sustained, a lesser person would not have survived this long. Even though she's unconscious at the moment, she stands a good chance of recovery."

"What were the injuries?"

"Well… extreme lacerations to various parts of her body, and…"

The pause was more than pregnant. "Please, it's all right. Go on."

"There was a lot of… tearing as well… bites, you know. But plastic surgery can do wonders these days. Really amazing things."

"Did the doctors give any indication when she might regain consciousness?"

"Could be hours or could be days they said. No way to be sure. Will you be coming down to be with her?"

"Uh… yes, but don't have a flight yet. Need to set that up."

"Having someone here will help enormously, I'm sure. Even if patients can't verbalize their thoughts, they can sense when someone who cares about them is close by."

"I'm sure that's true. Listen, Nurse Meyers, thanks so much. I may be calling again before I come down. I'll ask for you if that's okay."

"Certainly. And what is your first name, sir. For the record, you know."

"It's… John. John Carlyle. Like my sister."

"All right, I'll look forward to seeing you, John. Oh, and please do me a favor, if you don't mind."

"When you get here, please don't go into what we talked about over the phone. As I said, I'm not really supposed to provide information… but you being a relative and all."

"Don't worry. Won't say a word. Thanks again, and… oh, just one more thing?"

"What's that?"

"Did anyone happen to say what kind of animal attacked Car… my sister?"

"Not definitively, but due to the extent of the injuries there was a lot of speculation that it must have been a large animal, like a bear or a mountain lion. It's terrible for your sister, I know, but it's really a shame for the animal as well. I mean they just do what's instinctual you know. They don't react out of malice like people do. And you know what they say… once they get a taste of human flesh… well… Mr. Carlyle? John? Are you still on the line?"

THE MISSION...

CRACKED, CAKED, HARD GROUND HAD turned to sand. It was as if the earth were wasting away. And so were those crossing it. Tough men turning to mere shells of what they were when their supposedly quick in-and-out mission began. The sun was rising on their third day with no food or water. Exhaustion was taking its toll. Fowler was ill-tempered and irritable. Devlin kept having bouts of blurred vision. Adams struggled with things as minor as unbuttoning his tunic or tying his boot laces. Tasso was having piercing headaches. Ellis's judgment was becoming impaired. He had begun to debate with himself over rudimentary decisions like when to start, when to stop, what star or constellation to follow.

Sanchez was in the worst shape of all. It had begun with fainting spells. He would momentarily lose consciousness and simply drop to the ground as they walked. After the Corporal's second fall, Ellis had the men construct a field travois. Tunics were tied together to serve as the bed. Arms of the garments were knotted to rifles which became the poles. Sanchez was laid in the middle. The squad members would takes turns hefting each side and dragging it along. Even with the burden of walking taken away, Sanchez began to experience hallucinations. In his fevered imagination, the men pulling him along were burros, those marching behind became costumed skeletons in a macabre procession for Dia de los Muertos—The Day of the Dead. In ever-decreasing moments of lucidity, Sanchez wondered if they were in fact hallucinations or simply visions of their future. A future that included a new member of their squad... starvation.

The human body can only sustain itself for so long without some form of sustenance. The brain, deprived of energy begins to shut down. The heart can't pump as effectively as it should. The gastrointestinal system goes south. Bloating, nausea, and dry heaves begin. The absence of fat reduces testosterone. Thyroid hormones weaken bones. Even as the outside temperature increases, individuals temperatures decrease. The body virtually starts consuming itself. Ellis was keenly aware the starvation process had begun. But he and his men were completely surrounded by arid emptiness, and had gone too far to turn back.

"Let's pull up for a while," Ellis said.

No one had to be told twice. Devlin and Adams set the travois down and slumped to the ground beside it. Fowler crumpled as well. Tasso walked back to where Ellis was. They both walked a few steps from the others and let themselves down easily. Neither wanted the other men to hear their conversation.

Ellis formed it as a question, but it sounded more like a statement. "We're not going to make it, are we?"

"With no food plus no water, starvation comes sooner. Our bodies have begun to destroy us." Tasso replied.

"And the more ground we cover, the more we do ourselves in. Guess it's always been a race with the fix in. Why couldn't I see that there was no way to get across this thing before we died trying?"

"Don't second-guess yourself," Tasso said. "You made the right choice."

"Be honest, Sergeant. You see any way to do this?"

"How many more days to go?"

"Can't be sure. At least two or three," Ellis answered.

"The men can't do that, Lieutenant. The dying will start before then."

"Sanchez?"

"Surprised he's lasted this long," Tasso said.

"Me too. Nothing stronger than the instinct to survive, I guess."

"How strong is your survival instinct, Lieutenant?"

"What do you mean?"

"What are you willing to do to save as many as you can?"

"Whatever it takes, Sergeant. I assumed you knew that."

"You asked me if there was any way for us to make it. There is not… if we do nothing. But if we do something… there is at least a chance."

"What would that chance require?"

"Survival of the fittest."

"Sanchez?"

"One life for five."

"And we still might not make it."

"The only guarantee in life is death. It comes to us all. He will understand."

Ellis always knew the price of command was high. Apparently it was now time to pay the piper.

"And Lieutenant… death is not all that will be required of Sanchez… or us."

CHAPTER 11

IT HAD HAPPENED LIKE CARLYLE said it would. The unconscious mind, if stimulated sufficiently, would find what the conscious mind had been looking for. Words spoken willy-nilly by a talkative nurse had pushed the search-button in Ellis's brain and connections were starting to form, scenarios beginning to play out, next steps coming into focus. The first of which was the need to stay free long enough to follow potential premises without the authorities hamstringing him and slowing the process. Recent events had shown all too clearly that lives depended on it.

The first, and most important thing he needed was cash. Multiple withdrawals from one or more ATMs wouldn't be enough. Plus, each time he'd use his ATM and take money from his account, he'd be leaving a trail for the police to follow. No, he needed lots of cash. Cash that would allow him to avoid using credit cards, the use of which could also be traced. Cash that could be employed to persuade desk clerks that he didn't really need to show them identification to get lodging, or transportation, or anything else that might aid him in securing answers to questions he hadn't completely thought through yet. He needed a lot of money fast, and he had only one way to get it. A way that, under any other circumstances, he would never consider. But good people had been killed. One was fighting for her life even now. And like it or not he was right in the middle of it. He didn't like it. Not one damn bit. But he was committed.

After cleaning himself up and packing his kit bag—which included making sure he had at least two full clips for his Glock that Carlyle had forced Ordona to return—Ellis drove into a secluded residential section of Sedona and spent the night in his car. It was the kind of neighborhood he had been looking for. Upscale enough to avoid loitering miscreants yet downscale enough to infrequently get patrolled. The next morning he was at his destination bright and early. The minute the automobile dealership opened Ellis drove in. He reasoned there was no better place to hide a distinctive car than on a lot full of distinctive cars. The conversation didn't last long. Ellis was willing to accept a lot less if the dealer agreed to pay him in cash. He made a quick trip to his bank while Ellis sat in the guy's office and drank coffee. Less than an hour and a half from pulling in, Ellis was in a taxi with an ache in his heart and thirty-five thousand dollars in his bag. His melancholy wouldn't last long, however. It would soon be supplanted by maneuvers, as the hunted was about to become the hunter.

THEY SLEPT DURING THE DAY as they had been doing. But when twilight turned to night, instead of getting the men on their feet and heading out once more, Ellis had Tasso take them away from the travois and told them to continue resting. They were more than happy to comply.

When Sanchez and Ellis were alone, and the Corporal was again conscious, Ellis said, "Still with us?"

"I guess. Where are the guys?"

"They're just over there. Taking a break."

"Bet they need it. Must be a bitch hauling me around on this thing."

"How do you feel?"

"Awful, Lieutenant. Just awful. I've shit and pissed myself," Sanchez said, a tear emerging in the corner of his eye.

"We're all in the same boat. Don't give it a second thought."

"I'm sorry I got knifed sir. And became such a burden. Should have shot the moment I saw her."

"Not your fault. This mission's been fubar from the get-go."

"Fucked beyond all recognition, my favorite..." his mouth stopped as his mind drifted away from his train of thought.

"Sanchez? Sanchez?" Ellis put his hand on the Corporal's shoulder. It seemed to bring him back from wherever he'd been.

"Sanchez, Sergeant Tasso and I have been talking. He doesn't think we can make it as things stand. If we can't get through to the border in the next two or three days, we'll all be dead."

"Tasso knows his shit. He's an Indian, you know."

"The thing is... we can't get two more days... maybe even one more day.... hauling this travois. No matter how often we spell each other, the guys just can't do it. They're too exhausted."

Sanchez looked Ellis in the eye. "It's okay, Lieutenant. I know where you're going with this... Hell, I always wanted to be the guy who saved everybody else."

Now the tears were in Ellis's eyes. "If there were any other way, Corporal. Any way at all..."

"I know, Sir."

"If we do make it, and that's a big if... it will be because of you."

"Will you help me, Sir?"

"Sergeant Tasso will. He's more skilled than I. He promises you won't feel a thing."

"I can't feel a damn thing now, Lieutenant." Then the soldier gazed up at the stars in the night sky." How about that, Lord... Corporal Juan Antonio Sanchez, a by-god hero."

There was no need to tell him what else was deemed necessary. So Elli simply squeezed the young soldier's hand, rose and walked toward the group. Tasso saw Ellis nod. He got on his feet, went to Sanchez, knelt beside him, and spoke.

"For the smallest guy in the squad, amigo, you got bigger balls than any of us. Let your spirit soar," the Apache said, as he used his knife to open Sanchez's vein at one wrist, then the other.

CHAPTER 12

WHEN ELLIS HAD INITIALLY LEARNED of Tasso's death, the mission that the former Lieutenant had been able to lock away in the far reaches of his mind, made its way back. But initially there seemed no reason to assume one had anything to do with the other. Then, as one killing followed another, it became apparent to Ellis that someone, for some reason, was definitely trying to place the blame on him. Yet even that didn't knot his former mission to his current situation. Why would it? Why would something that had happened so many years ago have any connection whatsoever? No. It wasn't until the loquacious Nurse Meyers blurted out her oft-used phrase about crazed carnivores getting a taste for humankind that Ellis began to reflect on the possibilities that lay before him. Could any of the men involved then, be involved now? Sanchez and Tasso were dead. Only Adams, Devlin, and Fowler remained. And he didn't know if they were above ground or not. The horror they all went through had cemented their past but not their future. As was so often the case, the tactical squad was dismantled upon their return, promises were made to keep in touch, but no one did. Perhaps in each of their hearts, they knew that seeing one another—regardless of how much time might pass in between—would only be a reminder of what they all so desperately wanted to forget.

ADAMS, FOWLER, AND DEVLIN SPRAWLED on the ground too weak to open their eyes or even attempt to turn over. Ellis sat beside them, his head in his hands, while yards away in the darkness, Tasso worked as meticulously as muscle and mind numbing fatigue would let him. It took more than an hour for him to prepare. When he returned to where the other men were, he willed his legs to bend enough to ease himself down. Ellis immediately took note of his Sergeant. The Apache now had a single horizontal line across his forehead. It was red. Blood red. And in front of him, he placed a tunic, folded precisely to cover its contents, and a helmet half-full with dark liquid.

"It is time," Tasso said to Ellis, who moved over and gently shook the other three soldiers awake.

"A little while longer?" Devlin asked.

"Not time yet. Not time." Fowler grumbled.

Adams simply rubbed his eyes without speaking.

"Listen, men. I want you to listen to me," Ellis began. "I want you to hear what I'm saying."

Each man tried his best to train his consciousness on Ellis, but even listening had become an ordeal. Still, they paid attention as best they could.

"We're all exhausted. With no way to recharge. Each of us

is starving, with no sustenance to refuel. Each of is going to die if we don't do what we have to do to keep going."

The three looked at Ellis intently. They had no idea why he was saying all that he was.

"Sergeant Tasso… and I… and Corporal Sanchez… are not going to let us all die. We're going to walk out of this hell on our own two feet. To do that, we have to put away our inhibitions. We have to put away anything that might keep us from doing whatever we have to do to stay alive. Can you do that?"

The three looked at each other, then Tasso, eventually back to Ellis. They nodded their heads and mumbled as best they could, "Yes, sir."

"Tonight," Ellis said, "we regain our strength… we reinstate our will… we choose to survive." Motioning to Tasso, he said, "Sergeant."

Tasso slowly unfolded the tunic in front of him. The three looked at it unbelieving. Could it be? Were they dreaming? Was it hallucination? Were they actually seeing strips of meat?

Chicken? Snake? Boar? What was it?

"Where did you get that?" Fowler asked Tasso.

Devlin quickly followed, "Did you manage to kill something?"

Adams looked at all around him, "So what are we waiting for?"

Tasso spoke, "One has sacrificed so that all might live."

Again they looked at each other. Then it began to get through to them.

Devlin asked, "Where's Sanchez?"

Fowler said, "Wait a minute, that's not… no. Hell, no."

Adams simply stared glassy-eyed, his mouth agape but emitting no sound.

Tasso said, "To not partake, would be an affront to one who gave everything so you might live."

A stunned silence remained. The men seemed locked, spellbound. Ellis realized it was up to him. "I give thanks, and chose to live," Ellis said, as he reached down, took a strip of flesh, and bit into it.

"I give thanks, and choose to live," Tasso said, who did the same.

Adams bent, rubbed his hand across his mouth, and repeated, "I give thanks and choose to live."

Then Devlin. Then Fowler. In their insatiable hunger, they ravenously consumed the only thing they'd had to eat for days. As they did, they said nothing, overcome by wonder and horror and grief. The helmet was passed round and each put aside revulsion to coat parched lips and sandpaper throats. The more they consumed, the more they were engrossed in what had been done for them. Fowler began to tell stories of the Latino's prowess and chutzpa in the face of danger. Devlin spoke of the little man's grit and determination. Overcome with emotion at the gift of life they had received, and their temporary reprieve from the long sleep of death, gallows humor seemed the only way to keep their sanity. Fowler looked from one to the other and said, "Hey fellas, come on. Don't think of it as Sanchez... think of it as... Mexican food." None wanted to laugh, but they couldn't help themselves. Chortles became snickers. Snickers became giggles. Giggles became cackles. Cackles became guffaws. Raucous laughter rose into the sky and shattered the silence of the night around them. Then, when it had become virtually impossible to laugh any longer, each man silently wept.

CHAPTER 13

ELLIS KNEW HE WANTED TO forget what the squad went through. But he also knew it was impossible. Maybe one of the remaining members felt the same way. Maybe one of them wanted to forget so much that he was determined to wipe out all vestiges of the squad itself. Or maybe one blamed his Lieutenant for everything that happened. There's no statute of limitations on Post Traumatic Stress Disorder, Ellis mused. It could sit dormant for years, then begin to manifest itself in ways that less troubled minds could never imagine. Could it be that one of the remaining members of the squad had become so deranged that he'd started a killing spree that might not have an end in sight?

The P.I. did his best to punch his memory rewind button. Was there something about one of the three that might have foretold such violent mayhem? Violence was at the heart of their jobs. It was what they signed up for. Did one of them like it more than the others? They all volunteered to be Army Rangers. They were all hand-picked for search and destroy missions where taking lives rather than prisoners was standard operating procedure. Had one of them been unable to stop?

Ellis sped through his internal memory loop. What were they really like? None had been in the army very long, Ellis remembered, and even though they were volunteers, he didn't think any of them planned to make a long-term career of the service. Devlin could be a bit of a loner, Ellis recalled. More into religion than most at that time. Wore a rosary around his neck. Kidded—at least Ellis thought he was kidding—that it not only kept the bad guys at bay but that it also kept him from letting sin get the best of him. Fowler gave off the toughest vibes. A Black guy from Georgia, he seemed more wary than most about being friends with his fellow soldiers. The army prides itself on being color blind, Ellis reflected, encouraged by his superiors to frequently repeat the trope, *"Everybody in this army is the same color, O. D. [olive drab] Green."* He knew Fowler heard that a lot, but Ellis wasn't completely sure he believed it. And Adams, well, Adams was actually the easiest to forget. Did his job. Didn't complain. Didn't make waves. An integral part of a well-oiled team. But Ellis was damned if he remembered much else about him.

There were three left, not counting himself, of the six-man squad. Six men who went on a mission to make a quick entry, lethal attack, and swift exit. It was all supposed to have been over in hours. Completed and forgotten. Now years later, it had taken up residence in Ellis's head like it was yesterday.

AFTERWARDS, WHILE IT WAS STILL dark and before the sun would make it impossible to expend the energy, the squad buried Sanchez as best they could. Knives stood in for spades they didn't have to burrow enough sand away to cover him. No one spoke aloud. Each knew what the Mexican had done for them and each thanked him in a personal, but silent way.

There wasn't a lot of darkness left until dawn, but all wanted to put distance between themselves and what they had done. So they walked, as they had been doing for days. Walking north and willing themselves to keep putting one foot in front of the other, to keep moving each leg steadily ahead, to keep convincing themselves that they would somehow get where they were going before the sun and the earth and the cloudless sky simply swallowed them.

Heat plays tricks on the eyes. Especially when those eyes and every other part of the body have gone beyond the breaking point. Images in the distance take on a life of their own. One thing can look like another. Mirages can seem incredibly real even when they aren't. But then, sometimes they are real.

Tasso saw it first. Saw it, but wasn't ready to believe it. He used the back of his hand to rub his eyes, afraid that using his fingers would simply implant more sand. When he stopped, the others did as well. Ellis walked to where the Apache was standing.

"What's the matter, Sergeant?"

Tasso didn't speak, he simply pointed.

Ellis looked down the length of the man's arm and then in the direction his finger was aimed. The horizon was there, as it had been for days. But there was something wrong with it. It wasn't brown. It wasn't flat. It wasn't endless. Something rose from the horizon line. Something tall, and green, and fertile. My God, Ellis thought. It was what it actually appeared to be. The end of The Empty Quarter. The border. They were going to make it.

In their unbridled, yet exhausted joy, Ellis and Tasso simply reached out and put a hand on each other's shoulder. But then, before turning to see if they rest of the men were aware of what was in front of them, a realization came to Ellis.

"We were closer than we thought."

The Apache understood the real meaning of his Lieutenant's words.

"There was no way to know."

"He might have made it. We might not have—"

"You made the right decision," Tasso said, "for all of us."

"But…"

"Take the point, Lieutenant, and lead your men to safety, I'll take the rear."

Before the sun dropped from sight that day, the squad crossed the border.

CHAPTER 14

THE KEY WAS THE SQUAD, Ellis told himself. It had to be. Whether the impetus was a PTSD break from reality, or a cold and calculated plan that had been simmering for years, the motive must be revenge, he reasoned. Revenge for the mission itself, or revenge for trying to cross on foot what none had ever crossed before, or revenge for what was done with Sanchez, or maybe even revenge for the fact that a night forever seared into each man's memory might not have been necessary at all if Tasso and Ellis had done a better job of predicting how much farther there was to go. Tasso and Ellis. Ellis and Tasso. Surely that's it, he began to convince himself. That's the reason Tasso's dead, and I'm being made to look like a murderer. In one of those guys twisted minds, killing Vic and turning me into a pariah is somehow justifiable. Or, Ellis took his ruminations even further, maybe it's all three, teaming up to finally get back at Vic and me. He didn't really put much stock in that scenario, but like Carlyle said, "You need to consider every possibility, or you might miss something."

Motive was one thing, but it wasn't the only thing Ellis contemplated as the Jeep Cherokee with the Uber sign affixed to the door made its way to the destination the P.I. had given the driver. What about opportunity? What about the fact that someone, or someone doing someone else's bidding, had to be tracking Ellis's every move? Or at least he was in Santa Fe. Then again on the Yavapai Reservation. What about now? Was someone continuing to follow him now? Or had the attack on Carlyle, followed by his subsequent dodge and leap off the grid, slipped the tail that had been following him? Too soon to know for sure, he thought, but not too soon to look for the individuals he had moved to the front of his suspect list.

The Crimson Crystal was a combination coffee shop, T-shirt store, and Internet Café. Ellis had come for the technology, not the java or the sweatshirts reading Sedona, Older Than Dirt. He had his laptop with him but was hesitant to use it. Internet protocol addresses can be tracked. Authorities have ways of running down an individual's Internet Service Provider and convincing the entity to reveal one's computer IPA. Once that's done, it isn't long before every place the person goes, every site he views is disclosed to the cops. Ellis wasn't in the mood to share just yet.

At the keyboard of one of the customer desktops, he started with what he remembered about the trio and where they were from, which was very old and much too general. And while he assumed none of them were still in the service, that was still a place to start a historical search by name, rank, and time frame, then work his way forward. Morning turned to afternoon and then to evening as trial and error became trial and error and error and even more error. But perseverance was hard-wired into Ellis's DNA, and by nightfall he had collected eight Robert Devlins from Massachusetts, two Deets Folwers in Georgia, and ten Stephen Adamses in Nebraska. He decided he'd start with emails, then phone numbers when he could nail them down. Ellis was unconcerned about one or all of them knowing that he was now looking for them. The innocent wouldn't mind, and if the guilty did, "Fuck him," Ellis said to himself. But that was all work for the following day. This night he'd make only one call, which would be to Phoenix.

"Banner University Medical Center. How may I help you?"

"Nurse Meyers, please. In ICU."

"I will connect your call."

On the third ring, it was answered. "ICU. Nurse Meyers speaking."

"Nurse Meyers, this is John Carlyle," Ellis said. "We spoke last night. I was calling to see if there has been any change in my sister's condition."

"Oh yes. I remember. I'm afraid not, Mr. Carlyle. She's still breathing on her own but continues to be unresponsive."

"Have the doctors said anything more?"

"Nothing definitive. But they continue to believe there's a good chance she'll pull through. Will you be arriving soon? Even in her semi-comatose state, your presence would help, I'm sure of it."

"Yes. Soon. I will. But have to run now. Thank you."

"But…"

Once again Nurse Meyers stood at the Call Desk, receiver in her ear, hearing only a dial tone.

CHAPTER 15

STEPHEN ADAMS LOOKED AT THE email and found it hard to believe. Could it really be from his former Lieutenant, reaching out to him after all this time. What could he possibly want? The note didn't say. Just gave a phone number and asked for a call if he was the Stephen Adams who used to be an Army Ranger and volunteered for missions other grunts were running away from. He was. And he remembered Ellis using that phrase "missions other grunts were running away from." The Lieutenant had always been upfront about potential hazards involved, like death, dismemberment or both. He didn't try to trick anyone into volunteering the way some officers did. He was a stand-up guy, Adams thought. More so than most of the people he'd run into since leaving the service.

Adams had mustered out of the army with less conviction about what he was going to do with his life than when he went in. Making decisions was not his strong point. When it came to any real form of commitment, he was non-committal. That's why the one girlfriend he had managed to hold onto for more than a year decided she no longer wanted to be held. If he wasn't going to ask her to marry him, and it was obvious he wasn't, then she wasn't going to waste any more time in a relationship that didn't seem to have any future. And she didn't. She simply left a note on the rented (like the rest of the furniture in his apartment) dining room table. It read:

Stephen,
    You have no ambition. I do. That's why I'm leaving.
Don't call me.

He didn't. In his mind, she had more or less left an order, and he was good at following orders.

For the last few years he had knocked around from job to job. Security guard. Pipeline construction. Fork lift operator. Truck driver. He liked jobs with definitive objectives and precise instructions. Go here. Do this. Don't do that. Complete it by said time. From Adams' point of view, the best jobs were those you could walk away from at the end of your shift and not have to think about until you clocked in the next day. He didn't like jobs that required an over-abundance of thinking. He had enough to think about already with his girlfriend wanting out of his life and his old Lieutenant apparently wanting in.

Of course, any thought about Ellis, brought back thoughts of the mission they had all been part of. And particularly that one night. Though he had definitely tried, he'd never really been able to get it out of his mind. Sometimes it was just a quick recollection brought on by smell or taste. Sometimes it was a nightmare from which he couldn't seem to awake. Other times a daydream, when his mind wasn't fixed on a precise task. He wondered if his former Lieutenant thought about it too. He wondered if that's why Ellis was trying to reach him. Well, if it was, he'd find out tomorrow when he'd call the number in the email. It was too late to call tonight. Especially since he planned to get up early the following morning and do some fishing at the lake. Fishing was good. Fishing forced him to keep his mind on what he was doing. Fishing kept him from drifting into thoughts better left buried.

The next morning Adams was at the lake early. He never took a boat out, just strolled half-way around the lake and fished from the bank on the far side. The side closest to the woods. The sun had yet to rise when Adams's first cast plinked the surface, skimmed a few drops of water into the air, then silently sank to his chosen depth amid the rocks and reeds below. He kept a sharp eye on his Rod-N-Bobbs Original Glow Bobber that enabled him to fish before light spread its first rays across the lake's placid surface. So intense was his concentration on the floating sphere that he never heard the footsteps behind him, or the rush of air that foretold a mighty paw slamming down and into the back of his neck. A paw that sent a taser-like shock deep enough into Adams that he crashed to the still dew-soaked earth. Paralyzed, he was unable to move or cry out as the initial attack brutally progressed to final kill.

CHAPTER 16

ELLIS HAD CHOSEN TO SPEND the night at the lowest-profile motel he could find. One where he could pay in cash and for a few extra dollars keep his name off the register while keeping the desk clerk's memory faulty if official inquiries were made. The Starlight Inn fit the bill. No pool. No room service. No daily housekeeping. Not even a vending machine. Ellis decided to sleep on top of the bedspread, having no desire to crawl between the somewhat discolored and highly questionable sheets. He also kept his socks on to avoid direct contact between bare feet and shag carpet that harbored who knew what. The next morning he was up early, in another Uber, and on his way to a different location for both variety and caution. Cosmos Connection advertised coffee and connectivity so he settled on that particular Internet Café for both.

Having received no phone calls since leaving his initial email, and since Adams began with an A, Ellis decided to start there. He had a vague memory of the soldier once telling him that he was from Omaha. With that tidbit in mind, he Googled 'largest newspaper in Omaha,' and was quickly given the URL for the *Omaha World-Herald*. Checking the recent obituaries seemed a reasonable first step in light of all that had been going on, but he never got to the obits. When the landing page came up, he couldn't avoid seeing the forty-point banner reading: **Breaking News Headlines**. Just below it was a twenty-four point subhead that read: **Bear Kills Local Fisherman**. A quick scan of the copy beneath the bold type gave the approximate time the body was found, the location, a ghoulish description of the severity of the wounds, and the name of the individual found on the driver's license in the wallet of the deceased, Stephen Adams.

"Jesus," Ellis involuntarily said out loud. Then he added what he had just learned to what he had previously assumed and it came out bad news, good news. The bad news was Adam's death. One more former squad member eliminated. The good news? The killer obviously wasn't trailing Ellis at the moment. He had moved on. But that could be even worse news for Devlin and Fowler because the timing of Adam's death indicated the killer already knew where the ex-soldiers were or where they would be. Chances are he had the same intel on Devlin and Fowler that he had on Adams. Were that the case, both of their lives would be in imminent danger as well. Then Ellis realized it was also possible that one of the two remaining soldiers could be behind everything that had happened. The P.I. found himself on the uncomfortable horns of a potentially deadly dilemma. If he could locate Devlin and Fowler to warn them about what he thought was happening... and if one of them really was responsible... he'd be telling the actual killer everything he knew. *Too damn bad*, he told himself. It was worth it to try and help whichever one was innocent, or both, or neither if they were somehow in it together. But he still didn't believe the latter to be the case. Ellis continued putting his bet on PTSD and an irresistible urge for revenge, which in his mind, were non-communicable diseases.

Just as he was about to dive back into another hardcore

cyber search, the phone with the number he had sent out in earlier emails rang.

"Hello?"

"Hello?"

"Who is this?" Ellis asked.

"Who is *this*?" The caller said.

"This is Brig Ellis. Ex-Lieutenant Ellis?"

"Lieutenant? Is that really you?"

"Yes. It's really me," Ellis answered, as he ran his fingers down his notes, as yet still unsure of who was really on the other end of the call. "Devlin? Is that you. Do I have the right Robert Devlin?"

"Yeah. I'm Robert Devlin. Ex-Army Ranger like you asked in your email. I thought this might have been some kind of phishing hoax. I almost didn't call."

"Well, I'm glad you did, Devlin. I've got some things to tell you that you might find hard to accept. But I hope you'll believe me, because the truth is… your life may well depend on it."

CHAPTER 17

ROBERT DEVLIN'S LIFE SINCE LEAVING the military had been anything but dangerous. His last mission, the one he could never quite get over, left him with an intense desire to purge anything and everything that seemed the least bit risky, hazardous, or threatening from his modus operandi. He had come back from service to his country with an innate desire to somehow atone for the things he had done. Devlin had seriously considered entering the priesthood, but in his heart he knew he'd never be able to cope with the demands of celibacy. Still he longed to somehow make amends for assignments he'd undertaken voluntarily, orders he'd followed blindly, and actions he'd participated in that left death in their wake. He knew the individuals he'd personally eliminated with extreme prejudice were the worst of the worst. Yet he still felt remorse for what he had done to his foes and particularly for what he had done with his comrades on that awful night. A night that never seemed to be totally purged from its place in his mind.

Even though Devlin knew he would never become an actual priest, attachment to the Catholic Church became an obsession. He joined a parish just outside Boston and began a concerted effort to learn all that he could about church doctrine while volunteering for whatever work was needed to help the poverty stricken, house the homeless, and bring more souls into the bosom of the church. Such was his commitment, energy, and enthusiasm, that he was eagerly sought for salvific work not only by the priests in his diocese but the bishop as well. It was therefore not surprising when Robert Charles Devlin was named a Lay Ecclesial Minister and began actual employment supporting operations of the church's pastoral staff. A former soldier for the army whose job was raining down hell and damnation was now a soldier for God offering salvation to lost and lonely souls.

Devlin had listened to Ellis's explanation of what happened to Tasso and Adams, as well as his conjecture about the possible cause of it all. He found it almost impossible to believe. "Such good men," he said, "come to such a terrible end. And you really think Fowler had something to do with it?"

"He's the only one from the squad left. Not counting you and me. Of course, if you have something you want to tell me… something you might want to confess."

"Believe me, Lieutenant, I had nothing to do with what you've told me. I could never take another life. Not since I've committed myself to the church. And as for what happened that night, well, I know you and Tasso were just trying to keep us alive a few days longer. I believe you did what you thought was best to save the squad."

There was no way to know for sure whether Devlin was being sincere. Ellis had to go with his gut instinct. "Look, Devlin. I believe you. And if it is Fowler, he must be totally out of his head. You know as well as I do that there's no time limit on things going haywire in someone's brain. The key thing for now is that you watch yourself. Stay alert. Don't go off on any jaunts in the woods or the hills or whatever there is outside of Boston, okay? Keep your eyes open and pay attention to everything around you. When I find out more, I'll get back to you. Is the number you're calling from okay to reach you?"

"It is. And I'll be careful, Lieutenant. Thanks for running me down. Sorry it had to be under such terrible circumstances. You take care of yourself too. I mean it sounds like you're potentially in more trouble than anyone."

"It is what it is. But I intend to change that. And obviously, if you do happen to see Fowler… give him a wide berth… don't engage. And let me know soonest, okay? At this same number."

"Will do, Lieutenant. And thanks again."

"I'll get back to you. Take care."

After the call, Devlin found it difficult to get the images Ellis had described out of his head. He found it hard to believe that Fowler had gone off the deep end like that. Sure, he had been standoffish, and a bit of a loner. Not as friendly as the other guys. But a killer of his old mates… that was hard to accept.

I'll be vigilant, Devlin said to himself. *I'll keep to my regular routine.* Which included bringing potential believers into the fold. He had met one only hours before his call with Ellis. A fellow he thought perhaps he had seen somewhere in the past, but just couldn't place him. An individual who told him he was definitely down on his luck and looking for a way to turn his life around. There is a way through Christ and the church, Devlin remembered telling him. Just as he remembered the time of the appointment they had set up that afternoon to show him the cathedral where they would meet a priest who could provide the first steps in absolution of his sins. This was a soul that could be saved, and that's what Devlin did now. It was his vocation. He helped bring the lost into the light of salvation. How could he possibly know that within a few short hours, on that very day, he'd be letting the wolf in the door.

CHAPTER 18

ELLIS REALIZED THERE WAS NO way to be one hundred percent certain that Devlin was telling the truth. If he was, then at least his ex-squad member had been warned and hopefully he'd look out for himself. If Devlin was lying, and actually was the killer, Fowler would be the one in danger. Either way, Ellis wanted to make contact. So he plunged back into his internet search that had turned up two Deets Fowlers in Georgia. To move from an internet address to a phone number or even better, an actual street address, Ellis realized the cash he carried in his kit bag wouldn't be of immediate help. He'd have to use his credit card on a proper identity search site and take a chance on being tracked. If he got what he needed, he'd be out the door with no plan on returning to the Cosmos Connection. If he didn't, things might get dicey. But that was a chance he was willing to take.

A half-hour later, he had two numbers to call. He would need them both.

"Hello."

"Hello. Is this Deets Fowler?"

"Yes. Who is this?"

The voice didn't sound at all like the voice of the Black soldier Ellis remembered, but he had to be sure. "Is this the Deets Fowler that used to be an Army Ranger?"

"No. You must have the wrong number."

It definitely wasn't the voice. "Sorry, my mistake," Ellis said, then abruptly hung up.

The second call was infinitely more interesting.

"Yo."

Different way to answer the phone, Ellis thought.

"Is this Deets Fowler?"

"Who wants to know?"

"I'm an old friend of his. We were in the army together. Is this you, Fowler?"

"No, this ain't no Fowler. No swinging dick gets to talk to Mr. Fowler that don't talk to me first."

"Okay. I'm talking to you first. But I'm trying to talk to Deets Fowler. The Deets Fowler who was an Army Ranger. Is he there? Can I talk to him? It's very important."

"I'll decide what's important, asshole. You tell me."

"I need to talk to him directly. It's literally a case of life or death."

"Whose?"

"His."

"Hell, Mr. Fowler's life is up for grabs every day, man. You gonna have to do better than that."

"Look," Ellis began, trying to keep his temper in check, "if Mr. Fowler finds out that I tried to call and warn him, and you kept me from getting through… I have a feeling there's going to be hell to pay and you'll be the one paying."

"What's your name, *ofay*?"

"Ellis. Brig Ellis. He knew me as Lieutenant Ellis."

"Well, I know you as pain-in-the-ass Ellis. Your call interrupted my nap. Now it's disturbing my whole fuckin' day. Anyway, Mr. Fowler ain't here now."

"Do you expect him back soon?"

"He'll be back when he gets back. That's the way he rolls."

"Listen, where you are now, is that like a business or what?"

"Mr. Fowler don't like nobody puttin' his business in the street, you know. I mean this thing you callin' 'bout… if it's stripper business, that's one thing… but if it's his other business, that's a whole 'nother thing."

"You sure you don't know when he'll be back?"

"Yes, I'm sure. Might be today, tonight, tomorrow, or next week."

"Okay, listen. Can you give him a message?"

"Do I sound like a kiss-ass messenger. Just call back, cracker."

"Look, just tell him I called, okay. Lieutenant Ellis. He can call me back at this number."

"He don't call people back, dude. People call him back."

"Important man, huh? Bet you wouldn't want to piss off an important man like that."

"Neither would you, if you know what's good for you, whitey."

"What's good for me is to talk with Fowler. I can do that over the phone or face-to-face. If it's the latter, then you and I might have a little conversation as well."

"Oh, want to dance with me, do you? Well, come on down to Hotlanta and we'll see if you're combat-ready or just another parade-ground pussy."

"Just, give the message to Fowler, okay. Ellis. Lieutenant Ellis."

"Kiss my ass, mofo. Mr. Fowler don't talk to nothin' less than a General."

The line went dead.

CHAPTER 19

DEETS FOWLER HAD ALWAYS BEEN a bit of a loner, and in the tough Atlanta neighborhood he grew up in, that was hard to do. There was always this or that gang recruiting, looking for young neophytes they could pull in, intimidate, then mold into unthinking followers. Fowler, however, was a thinker. He didn't put his intellect on hold for anyone. And it didn't take much ruminating to realize that agreeing to be part of the Rollin' '60s Neighborhood Crips, the Diablos, or the Stone Gangsta Bloods, was basically a one-way ticket to prison or the cemetery. He wasn't in a hurry to get to either.

So when he was old enough to do so on his own, he left his neighborhood with its meth, marijuana, cocaine, and heroin, and signed on the dotted line with the United States Army. There, he could learn things that would stand him in good stead later in life. Not necessarily the kind of things the military talked about in recruiting commercials, such as technical knowledge, discipline, and interpersonal skills. No, the things he wanted to learn and become proficient at were more along the lines of escape and evasion, hand-to-hand combat, survivability and lethality. Those were the aptitudes he'd need when he returned to his old stomping grounds not to fit in… but to stand out. Not to sign on… but to take over. Deets Fowler wanted to learn how to be both a leader and killer of men. Not necessarily in that order. So the army built his body and honed his mind. Ranger training, followed by one dangerous assignment after another, gave him the kind of experience few people ever get or want. He became what he wanted to be: cool on the outside, deadly on the inside. When his hitch was up, there was no thought of re-enlistment. He was ready to put his training to work in the side streets, back alleys, and night clubs of Atlanta.

A week after he returned, Fowler took a job as a bouncer at Bodacious, a club that featured strippers, lap dances, loud music, expensive drinks, and unadvertised but available illicit drugs. He showed both skill and initiative in removing unruly patrons with maximum force but minimal disturbance. It wasn't long before the owner of Bodacious recognized that Fowler's intellectual gifts matched his physical prowess. He promoted the ex-soldier to assistant manager, then later to manager, then before he knew it, the tables decidedly turned. Fowler instigated and accomplished an in-house coup d'état that sent his boss packing, pissed off, but pleased to still be drawing breath and a small annuity that unbeknownst to him, Fowler planned to eliminate after the first installment. Bodacious was now Fowler's, and the neighborhood was soon to follow.

The phone rang. Ellis answered it. "Hello."

"Hey, Lieutenant Ellis, this is Deets Fowler."

"Fowler, thanks for calling me back. Long time, huh?"

"Yeah. Seems like forever."

Ellis wasn't sure if he was talking to an old mate, or a killer. He started cautiously. "Ever hear from any of the old squad?"

"Nah. I don't really keep up. Not the type, you know?"

"Well, guess you didn't hear, then?"

"Hear what?"

"Tasso's dead. Adams, too."

"Really? Both of 'em? Kind of young to be dropping like that, ain't they?"

"They had help."

"You don't say. Tell me about it."

Ellis felt at this point he had nothing to lose by opening up to Fowler as he had to Devlin. The ex-soldier's reaction might give him some indication of whether he was involved or not. Two minutes later, after going over what had transpired, but leaving out his theory about PTSD inspired revenge, Ellis was no closer to illumination.

"Well," Fowler began. "Sounds like somebody's definitely got it in for you and our old running mates. Maybe I should be watching my back even closer, huh?"

"You should. That's why I got in touch with you."

"I appreciate that. Hey listen, if you ever get down Atlanta way, stop in at my club, Bodacious. You'll have some fine ladies to look at and I'll even comp your drinks. Just a little something for old times, you know?"

"Just might take you up on that," Ellis answered. Then he tried one more gambit. "A club like that must keep you pretty anchored down, I bet. No chance to get away much?"

"Oh, I got a few guys here I can depend on. So I take a few days to myself now and then. Just got back from up north, actually."

"Oh, yeah. Where abouts?"

"New England. The Boston area. Mixing a little export-import business with pleasure."

"You don't say..."

"Listen, Lieu... I mean, Ellis. I understand you might have called earlier and talked to Maurice. He said things got a little chippy on the phone. Don't mind him. He gets paid to be intimidating. That's his job. Gets carried away with it every now and then."

"No big deal. I know how some gatekeepers can be."

"Okay, then. Well, I have to run now. Just got back and there's lots to do. Thanks for the heads up, man. I appreciate that. I'll watch out. You do the same."

"Will do."

"Over and out."

"Take care."

Ellis ended the call but didn't put down the phone. So Fowler had been near Boston, he reflected. Was there anyway Devlin would have known about that? If so, was there any reason he would not have mentioned it? Surely not. But he wanted to make sure. He dialed the number Devlin had used to call him back.

"Hello."

Didn't sound like Devlin's voice, Ellis realized. "I was trying to reach Robert Devlin. Is he there?"

"Were you an acquaintance of Mr. Devlin?"

Ellis immediately recognized the past tense. "I'm an old friend of his. Has something happened? Is he there? I'd like to talk to him, please."

"I'm very sorry to have to tell you this over the phone… you being an old friend and all, but Mr. Devlin is dead."

CHAPTER 20

THE VOICE ON THE END of the line, which later revealed itself to be Father Wainwright, didn't have all the details of what had happened or the exact cause of death. He simply said what Ellis had heard multiple times. The authorities think that some animal may have gotten into the rectory near the church and attacked Devlin. Ellis's thoughts immediately turned to Fowler admitting he'd been in the Boston area. He had now thought enough and heard enough. It was time to confront Deets Fowler—on his home turf if he had to—and the more he thought about Tasso and Bevel and her ex and Adams and Devlin… the more he knew he definitely had to. But first, he'd check on Carlyle. He prayed that her name hadn't already been added to the list of the dead.

"Hello. This is Nurse Meyers. Who's calling, please?"

"It's Ms. Carlyle's brother, John. I wanted—"

"You're not her brother," she said angrily. "The police verified that she has no siblings. Who are you? I bet you're the man they're looking for. The one that was with her."

Once again, Ellis picked up on the tense. She said has, not had. "She's still alive, right? Has she regained consciousness? Has she been able to speak?"

"You think I'm going to tell you? The authorities believe you're the one that hurt her."

"Please, Nurse Meyers, trust me. I had nothing to do with her being attacked. I'm trying my hardest to find out who did. Yes, I lied to you initially, but that was only because I wanted to find out if she was okay… if she was going to make it. I didn't think you'd tell me unless you thought I was a relative."

"But you—"

"I swear I had nothing to do with hurting her. Please, is she okay… or is she going to be okay."

"Oh…" Her conflict between believing the voice on the phone and doing what the police asked was giving her a fit. She decided to try and have it both ways. "Look, I'll tell you, but I'm also going to tell the authorities you called again."

"No problem. Just fill me in."

"Well, her vital signs have returned to normal. She's actually opened her eyes and made contact with the doctors and nurses. But she hasn't spoken yet. The doctors don't want to rush her, so the police haven't been allowed in."

"But you think she's going to be okay?"

"Well, I'm not a doctor, but she's definitely trending in the right direction."

"Thank you so much, Nurse… I don't even know your first name."

"It's Florence."

"Like Nightingale, right? Thank you so much, Florence. Hopefully, I won't have to bother you again soon. Or put you in a tough position with the cops."

"Oh, I'm not… you know, I mean… you can actually call back if you ask for me."

"They asked you to try and keep me on the line, right? So they could trace the call?"

"No. Well, actually, yes. But you sound so nice. I believe

you. I don't really think you would hurt Ms. Carlyle."

"You're right. Gotta go, Flo."

With that, Ellis broke the connection, put the burner on the floor, stomped it once, then picked it up and dropped it in the trash receptacle on his way out the door.

*   *   *

The Sedona Airport is a one-runway, towerless facility that sits atop a 500-foot mesa with spectacular 360° views of some of the most gorgeous scenery on the planet. Ellis had no time for sightseeing, however, as the Uber driver dropped him off at the front door. Once inside, he went directly to the counter and asked the clerk if there were any private planes available for charter. The clerk explained that there were and was about to hand Ellis a list with names and phone numbers to call. Ellis cut him short.

"No, I mean now," the P.I. said. "Is there a plane here now that's available?"

"Well, these operators don't usually do things on such short notice, you know."

"Can't help the timing," Ellis said. "Is anyone on this list available now? Or is there anyone else I could talk to."

"You understand that flight plans have to be filed and…"

Ellis zipped open his bag, reached in, and pulled out a hundred-dollar bill. "Anyone at all," he said, pushing the Benjamin halfway across the counter.

The clerk's attitude immediately went from cautious to conciliatory. "Well, there is… uh… Mr. Eisenstat."

"Does he have a plane?"

"He has a plane, but—"

"Where can I find him?"

"I believe he's out on the patio now. Enjoying a libation, as is his wont."

"How will I recognize him," Ellis asked.

"Just look for the hat and boots."

"Thanks," Ellis said. "Keep the change and a lid on our conversation, okay?"

"What conversation," the clerk asked, sliding the C-note into his drawer.

Ellis looked around and found the side door that lead outside to the patio. He took it and quickly spotted an individual leaning back in a chair with his feet propped on the chair opposite and his hat covering his face. The feet were wrapped in polished leather Tony Lama cowboy boots that showed not a bit of wear and tear. The fellow connected to them lounged under a grey Stetson devoid of sweat around the headband. His jeans were belted with a buckle the size of a bagel. He wore a black shirt with pearl snaps, and a suede jacket with three-inch fringe hanging off the sleeves. Ellis felt like he didn't need to ask, but he went ahead and posed the question.

"Is your name Eisenstat?"

The man tilted his hat back and pulled his Foster Grants down on his nose, revealing a lined face too old for the jet black eye brows and goatee, which were obviously more beholding to hair dye than age-defying genes.

"Who wants to know?"

"My name's not important."

"But mine is, huh? Guess that gives me the upper hand."

"More than happy to play it that way, just want to be sure I'm talking to the right man."

"Well sir, I am indeed Wild Bill Eisenstat, The Frontier Jew. No man like me before, after, or even as we speak. What can I do for you?"

"Like to charter your plane."

"What day?"

"Today."

"Where to? Phoenix? Flagstaff?"

"Atlanta."

"Don't believe I've heard of Atlanta, Arizona."

"Ever heard of Atlanta, Georgia?"

"Why not go commercial?"

"I have my reasons."

"What else do you have?"

"Cash."

"Counterfeit?"

"No."

"In that bag?"

"Yes."

"Illegal contraband?"

"No."

"Stolen goods?"

"No."

"Price sensitive?" Eisenstat asked.

"Depends," Ellis answered.

"On?"

"On whether we're going to waste time jawing all day or get on with it?"

"Mind showing me the goods?"

Ellis stepped closer, held the bag under Eisenstat's nose, unzipped it long enough to show multiple piles of bills and his Glock. "Price?"

"Let me see if I have this straight," Eisenstat began. "A man with no name... a man of mystery... seeks out The Frontier Jew, asking to be flown to the heart of Dixie post haste without benefit of flight plan, credit approval, or prior authorization...

is that about it?”

"Yep. How long? How much?”

"Round trip?”

"Probably just one way.”

"Ten hours. One stop to refuel. Total… ten thousand, five hundred.”

"Done. When can we leave?”

"Soon as we saddle up, amigo.”

CHAPTER 21

THE SILVER AND BLACK CIRRUS SR22 caught the glint of the sun as it lifted off and banked to the east. Soon it had leveled off at its cruising speed of a little under 200 miles per hour. While the engine was relatively quiet for a small craft, The Frontier Jew wasn't. Eisenstat had his hands on the controls, but when it came to regaling his passenger with his own personal history and tales of times gone by, the Hebrew drugstore cowboy's mouth was on autopilot. He told tall tales of violent run-ins with anti-Semitic skin heads, harrowing escapes from Baptist church groups intent on helping him be born again, and finding, losing, then finding again and losing again the love of his life, Noya Rosenbloom, who agreed to marry him, then at the last minute, left him the day before the ceremony to return to Israel and join the IDF in the fight against the Palestinians.

Ellis didn't feel the need to reciprocate with war stories of his own, but then he wasn't asked to. Eisenstat seemed more than content to listen to himself drone on without the need for mundane give and take that is found in most actual conversations. Occasionally, The Frontier Jew would tire, or need to take a breath, and such occurrences enabled Ellis to ask questions he was actually interested in.

"How we doing fuel wise?"

"Got enough to make this little FBO I know of in Tulsa. We can fill up and grab a bite to eat there."

Ellis said, "We didn't actually talk about what we'd do when we get near where we're going."

"I figured you'd get around to it when the time was right."

"You got a place you plan to set down?"

"Got a place I plan to *not* set down," Eisenstat answered. "That's anyplace near Hartsfield International. I get in their airspace and we'll be ducking FAA grand inquisitors for the rest of our natural lives."

"Just get me close enough to the city that I can grab a ride in. There must be Fixed Based Operators close by."

"There are. Says so on my handy-dandy Atlas. Plus, like any big city, I'm sure there are lots of farms and open fields that can make for a safe, if not somewhat bumpy landing."

The Tulsa FBO provided Avgas, coffee, and tuna fish salad sandwiches. It wasn't the lap of luxury but it was getting Ellis where he wanted to be without the Arizona or New Mexico cops trailing his every step.

After a long ride and about an hour out of Atlanta, Eisenstat popped the question. "You going to need a way back to Arizona?"

"Not sure, right now," Ellis answered.

"Time you get sure may be too late."

"Don't know how long my business is going to take. Why, you thinking about hanging around a bit?"

"Well, I'll have pockets full of your cash. Just might decide to check out the local color, you know. I'm kind of partial to peach cobbler, fried onion burgers, and Southern belles. If you're only going to be a day or two, I could take you back?"

"Not sure I can afford the return trip."

"Hell, I made a tidy profit on getting you here. I'm not the greedy type. Plus, you got me at a disadvantage, Kemosabe. Without someone in the passenger seat, I'd just have to dead-head back. That's a long ride without somebody to chew the fat with."

"Make me an offer, Ellis said."

"One thousand."

"Too high."

"Five hundred."

"Sorry."

"Three hundred."

"Two-fifty," Ellis countered.

"Sold at two-fifty, pardner. You drive a hard bargain."

"When we separate," Ellis began, "we'll exchange numbers. I'll call you when I'm ready to head back. If it's going to be longer than a day or two, I'll let you know and you can make your own decision about what you want to do." Then Ellis thought about just how complicated and hairy things might get. "And listen, if a day or two goes by and you can't get hold of me… make tracks, okay. No harm, no foul."

"I get your drift, outlaw. And if you happen to get into something you can't handle by yourself…" Pausing, Eisenstat reached under his seat and pulled out a forty-five-caliber Colt Bluntline Special with a twelve-inch barrel. "…don't hesitate to call in the calvary."

Ellis couldn't help but grin. "Wild Bill, you are a piece of work."

"Ain't it the truth?"

CHAPTER 22

THEY LANDED AT AN FBO twenty-five miles east of Atlanta. After exchanging phone numbers, Ellis caught a ride with one of the Operator's employees who had to drive into the city to pick up supplies. He had the fellow drop him off at a seedy looking motel that Ellis assumed would be amenable to cash in advance, no questions asked. His assumption proved correct. The P.I. wanted to grab a couple of hours sleep, a shower, and make himself at least somewhat coherent and passably presentable when he faced his old squad mate who just might have gone bonkers and may even be a stone-cold killer. Even though it was typically warm in Atlanta, he put on his jacket. Else his shoulder holster and Glock would be inappropriately brazen.

Ellis remembered the name of the club, Bodacious, from his phone call with Fowler. He called an Uber and when the midnight blue twenty-year-old Lincoln arrived, he told the driver where he wanted to go. Ellis was about to give the driver the address when the man behind the wheel cut him off, "Don't bother. I know where it is." Less than fifteen minutes later they pulled up in front of a one story building with faux Greek columns along the entryway, a huge neon sign reading "Bodacious" in green script, and flanked on each side of it, bouncing female breasts illustrative of the club's name. "I bring a lot of guys here," the cabbie said, accepting Ellis's fare and tip while passing him a business card with a phone number below copy that read: *Mo's Cab. Mo 4 U Dough.* "I'm Mo. Short for Mohammed. But don't spread it around. The local rednecks can get a little intense. Know what I mean? Give me a call if you need a ride later. I'm always somewhere in the neighborhood."

Stepping inside the club, Ellis found himself surrounded by mood. Low lights, intimate tables for two, plush booths, a bar running the length of one wall, and a circular stage occupied at the moment by a generously endowed Black girl slowly spinning round a floor-to-ceiling pole.

Scoping out the interior and looking, as he always did, for exits other than the one he had entered by, Ellis heard a girl speak before he turned and saw the petite blonde wearing a pair of horn-rimmed glasses and precious little else.

"Ten dollar cover charge, handsome."

"Oh, yeah. What do I get for my ten dollars?"

"You get to stay and spend even more money… if you're a good boy."

"Well," Ellis said facetiously as he handed her a ten-spot, "I am a good boy and I wouldn't want to miss an opportunity like that, would I?"

"Table? Booth?"

"I'll just grab a spot at the bar first," Ellis said.

"Suit yourself, sweet cheeks," the girl responded, adding as she walked away, "have a good time."

At the bar, Ellis ordered Woodford Reserve bourbon, neat. When the bartender, another scantily clad lass, set it in front of him she said, "Ten dollars."

Reaching in his pocket, Ellis quipped, "Seem to like Alexander Hamilton around here, huh?"

"We like Andrew Jackson and Benjamin Franklin a lot more. But Al's always good for a start."

Ellis took a sip of his whiskey and asked, "Is Fowler here?"

"Sorry, don't know him."

"That's odd. I have it on good authority he runs the place."

"Hey, Mister, I'm labor. I don't really know from management."

"Is anyone here who would?"

"You sure you want to ask."

"Come this far," Ellis said. "Might as well go all the way."

The pretty barkeep turned and picked up the receiver on a red phone just below the clear rows of vodka and gin. With her back to Ellis, she spoke into the phone less than ten seconds. Then she put the receiver down and turned back to him. "Just remember, you asked."

A door, flush with one wall of the establishment, opened and the light that came pouring out of it backlit an emerging hulk. Even from across the room, Ellis could tell the figure went 280 or 300 pounds easily. He guessed six foot five or six. As it came closer to him, Ellis was prepared to revise his estimate upward.

Towering over the P. I., who was still seated at the bar, the giant spoke. "You the one looking for Mr. Fowler?"

Ellis recognized the voice. "Your name wouldn't happen to be Maurice, would it?"

"How do you know my name?"

"We actually spoke on the phone. My name's Ellis. Remember, Lieutenant Ellis."

"Oh. Yeah," Maurice acknowledged, his surly attitude turning docile. "I gave you a hard time, didn't I?"

"You did."

"I was intimidating, wasn't I?"

"You were."

"That's what Mr. Fowler wants me to be. But he said I shouldn't have been that way with you."

"You didn't get in trouble, did you, Maurice?"

"A little. But a little of Mr. Fowler's trouble goes a long way. Does he know you're here?"

"Uh, no. Thought I'd just drop by and surprise him."

Turning toward the girl behind the bar, Maurice said, "Indigo, see if Mr. Fowler would like to see Mr. Lieutenant Ellis."

The girl went back to the red phone, spoke for only seconds, then said, "Yes. He said to take him on back, Maurice."

Ellis drained his glass, put it on the bar, and said, "Indigo, huh? That's a very pretty name."

"It's not mine. Mr. Fowler chose it. Said to use it and I'd get customers to talk more and buy more drinks."

"Mr. Fowler's a smart fellow. What's your real name?"

"Ida Mae."

"I'd stick with Indigo, if I were you," Ellis said, then rose and followed Maurice through the door in the wall, down a hallway, and up to a door with a sign on it that read: KNOCK BEFORE ENTERING... OR ELSE. Maurice did. Ellis heard Fowler shout.

"Come inside, Lieutenant. Maurice, you stay outside."

The big man opened the door for Ellis, let him pass, then closed the door behind him.

Fowler, seated behind a desk, rose as Ellis entered. The two men looked at each other silently. It had been years since one had seen the other. Years since Ellis had seen any of his former squad. While both were obviously older, there was still recognition, immediate recognition of who they once were, what they both used to be, and what they had gone through together. In that silent moment, Ellis found it hard to believe that the man in front of him could harbor enough hate, or psychic damage, to do the evil that had recently been done.

"So," Fowler spoke first, "you decided to take me up on my invitation. Didn't think it would be so soon."

"I didn't either, but events intervened and I thought it would be good if we talked."

"Sure, Lieu—damn, what the hell should I call you now?"

"Ellis would be fine. That's what everyone else calls me."

"Then have a seat." Fowler said, pointing to the two chairs in front of his desk as he sat back in his chair. "It's good to see you. It is."

There was little point in making their way through small talk. But they did anyway, with Ellis complimenting his ex-squad mate on the apparent success he had become in the industry euphemistically referred to as the entertainment business, and Fowler feigning interest in Ellis's private investigative work. Ellis, having already mentioned the events of the past weeks to Fowler on the phone, held off mentioning what he had learned about Devlin. At least until he had probed a bit more.

"You ever think about it," Ellis asked.

"Which it are you referring to?"

"That night. That last night before we reached the end of The Empty Quarter."

"No. I don't think about it. Well, at least I didn't until you just brought it up. Bugging you after all these years, is it," Fowler asked.

"It wasn't. Until all these deaths started," Ellis answered. "Now it seems to be hanging around like a sword of Damocles."

"Whoa... allusions to ancient Roman parables. Think I wouldn't know what you meant by that? Southern fried

Private Dumb as a rock? That what you think, Lieu—Ellis?"

"I didn't think. I was just talking off the top of my head. But since we're talking about it, what about you? You think I shouldn't have done what I did?"

"Hey, man. That's what officers are for. To make decisions. You made the call. We all followed you. Wanted any chance we could get to stay alive. Would we have made it without going savage and all? Hindsight says yes. But hindsight ain't worth dick when you're starving to death."

"So you don't hold it against me," Ellis asked.

"I might have for a while. More than one of us might have. But not now. Haven't you heard… time heals all wounds."

"Apparently not *all* wounds, or these deaths wouldn't be happening."

"You think it was one of us, huh? But according to what you told me, Tasso and Adams are dead. We both know Sanchez ain't involved unless he's come back from the grave to get us all. That only leaves Devlin and me. You think one of us is wreaking all this havoc?"

"Actually, it only leaves you. I got word that Devlin is dead. Killed like the others."

"Damn. That's a bitch." Then the unseen light bulb went off in Fowler's head. "Oh… now I see. You think this little Black boy from down South has been snuffin' all your badass ex-rangers. Is that it?"

"It's a possibility I had to follow up. Especially since you told me you were near Boston about the time Devlin was killed."

"So were millions of other people, I assume."

"Yes, but how many of those millions went through what we went through together. There has to be a connection. That's really why I came here. To try to decide if you're the killer… or maybe the next victim."

"Look, whoever's doing this better have the goddamned good sense not to try something with me. I don't go down easy."

"We both know Tasso didn't either. But he was the first to go."

That gave Fowler pause. He knew how well the Apache could take care of himself. Then he quickly bounced back to what Ellis had said earlier. "Okay, so I happened to be in a similar geography when Devlin got his. But let's get a little deeper into facts. Not just wild ass conjecture, okay? When were the others killed?"

Ellis laid out the dates and as he did, Fowler flipped through a desktop calendar that had notes written all over it. After doing so, the club owner was adamant that he'd been in Atlanta when Tasso, Bevel, and her ex had been killed… when Carlyle had been attacked… and when Adams was murdered.

"I suppose you can come up with witnesses for all those dates?"

"Ellis, in my business you can come up with witnesses for any damn thing you please. The point is I was here. Not somewhere off in New Mexico or Arizona or bumfuck Nebraska or wherever the hell Adams was done in."

It wasn't just the notes on a calendar. They helped provide support, but they could have been made any time. It was Fowler's attitude and adamancy that he was not involved that made Ellis think maybe he was aiming at the wrong target. *Damn it*, he said to himself. *If Fowler's telling the truth, that means my PTSD revenge-fueled motive is now just another dead end.* Still, he believed there had to be a connection. Bevel and her ex and Carlyle may well have been wrong place, wrong time, or merely collateral damage, or much more likely, additional fodder to paint Ellis as some psycho freak. But the killings of Tasso, Adams, and Devlin were really at the heart of it. Whatever the hell it was.

"Look, Fowler, let's say I believe you. Because, frankly, I do. But the point is, with the other guys dead, you and I are the only members of the old squad who are still alive. Whoever's doing this is trying to lay it all on me. Which also means you're in his crosshairs."

"Fuck him and the mule he rode in on. I told you what would happen if he comes for me."

"Yeah, you told me. But I'm not sure anyone's told him."

CHAPTER 23

WHILE THEY HAD BEEN TALKING, evening turned to night, and Fowler suggested going in to the club for something to eat. Having had little more than his in-route tuna fish sandwich recently, Ellis readily agreed. Fowler led him to a table that was always unoccupied and reserved for the boss. It provided a complete view of everything in the main room, which had filled substantially since Ellis arrived. Ninety-five percent of the crowd was male. Guys didn't bring dates to places like Bodacious. Unless the dates were curious enough to want to see what the club and the girls who worked there were like. This night only two had come to find out.

At Fowler's table the waitress asked, "What can I get you and your guest, Mr. Fowler?"

The owner turned to Ellis. "Up for a steak? We cut 'em lean and cook 'em mean down here."

"You're calling the shots," Ellis said.

"Burn two, darlin', black outside, red inside… kinda like me. Then tell Indigo we'll have a bottle of that Cabernet I like. She knows which one."

As Maurice stood beside the table and kept a watchful eye on the club, Fowler and Ellis reminisced a bit before and during their meal. The talk was about places they'd gone, things they'd done, people they'd served with… some, like them, who came out of it in one piece, some who didn't. Ellis asked if any of the guys who Fowler knew from the service ever came into his place.

"No. Not really. You're the only one… I think."

"You think?"

"Yeah. There was a guy in here a while back. A guy that looked familiar, but I really couldn't place him. Actually started over to ask if I knew him or if he knew me from somewhere, but by the time I crossed the room he had split."

Wait a minute, Ellis thought. Hadn't he heard something similar? What was it? Where was it? Yes, he realized, Santa Fe. The art studio where Tasso worked. The owner had mentioned Tasso seeing someone he thought he knew. That was it. The guy said Tasso went outside looking for him. Then came back saying he must have been wrong.

"What did this guy look like," Ellis asked.

"Just a guy, you know. White dude. Around our age. Couldn't place him. But it bugged me, you know. That's why I went over."

"And he was gone? You never actually talked to him."

"Naw. I didn't go outside. Didn't care that much about it. Just thought I knew him from somewhere. Wasn't like it was important or anything."

"Maybe it wasn't. Maybe it was. You have to assume that whoever's doing this has to do some planning up front. Reconnaissance, you know. Checking out the target before planning the assault."

"Yeah, but this was a good while back, man. You know, like weeks ago."

"An assassin with multiple targets has to order things accordingly. He has to put together an attack plan, even if he knows it may change over time. My movements may have altered his plans. I think I was able to lose him in Arizona and he probably reverted to his original schedule with Devlin. Which would put you next on his agenda."

"I do my worrying when the time comes," Fowler said, "not in advance. Waste less energy that way."

Once they'd finished, Ellis complimented the meal and the wine and when Fowler asked what his plans were, Ellis was noncommittal. He gave a vague answer about needing to work things out. If Fowler had been telling him the truth, he didn't want to get into a hassle over staying to help him look out for himself. If he'd been lying, he didn't want to be specific about what he'd do next. In point of fact, he wasn't sure anyway.

"Need a lift somewhere," Fowler asked.

Ellis remembered the card in his pocket. Pulling it out, he said, "No thanks. Driver said to give him a call."

"Driver have a name?"

"Mo."

"That's what I figured. Mo works this part of town a lot. Gets some extra pocket money from me every time he brings a fare over. Guys from out of town, don't know where to go for a good time, Mo brings 'em my way. Good business for me and for him. Give him a call. See if he's close by. If not, I can get you a ride."

Ellis called. Mo answered and said he'd be there in five minutes. Fowler offered to walk Ellis to the parking lot and get a breath of fresh air. Outside their conversation returned to the subject both knew they'd never truly put behind them.

"Sorry it's worked out the way it has," Fowler said. "The guys in the squad were okay. They didn't deserve to go like you told me. Hope you find the bastard and take him out."

"Just watch yourself, okay? This guy's a bad one… whoever the hell he is."

CHAPTER 24

MO'S LINCOLN SWUNG INTO THE parking lot and pulled over to where the two men were standing. The two said their goodbyes and Ellis got in the car while Fowler pulled a pack of cigarettes from his pocket to have a smoke and a walk around the club before going back inside.

"Back to the motel," Mo asked.

"Yeah, but first, let me check something, okay?"

"Sure, take your time," Mo said. Ellis pulled out the backup burner phone he was going to use to call and check on Carlyle. As he was retrieving the hospital's number, the relative silence of the night was shattered with one of the most ferocious growls Ellis had ever heard. Mo heard it too.

"What the hell was that?"

Wild barking and snarling continued unabated.

"Where's Fowler… the man I was with… did you see where he went?"

"He walked behind the club while you were looking for the number."

Ellis jerked open the back door, sprang out, and quickly pulled his Glock from its shoulder holster while running around the side of the building. He kept hearing snarling and grunting like a horrific animal fight was underway. Reaching the back, he realized it was.

But it wasn't two animals fighting. It was one animal and one man. Fowler was on the ground, held in a death grip on his forearm by a brown, barrel-chested pit bull. The massive canine was jerking his head from side to side and with it Fowler's blood-soaked appendage. Ellis was about to aim and fire when his peripheral vision caught sight of something standing just to the left of the melee. Something seemed the only appropriate noun. It stood on two feet, its body covered in buckskin, a beaver fur, or some sort of headdress covered its crown with strips of skin hanging down and upright horns protruding from each side. One arm was decidedly longer than its other and at the end of it a huge paw jutted forward with claws like that of a grizzly's fully extended. The other arm held some type of medieval mace with jagged objects like glass and metal plus actual teeth from different specimens in different sizes affixed to its business end.

Shocked, surprised, and still confused by what he was looking at, Ellis knew he had to separate the rabid dog from Fowler. He fired two quick shots in the air. The blasts scared the hell out of the thing standing next to the dog attack, but didn't do anything to halt the dog's aggression. The thing took off and ran like an Olympic sprinter toward the mustard field fifty yards from the club. Ellis wanted to give chase but knew he had to get the dog off Fowler. He raced as close as he could to the confrontation and pumped two quick slugs into the pit bull. The animal let out a high-pitched whine and released its jaws from Fowler's arm. Then it staggered and crumpled to the ground. When it did, Ellis stepped quickly beside it and fired a shot to the skull that ended the dog's assault once and for all.

Having heard the shots, Maurice and others came running from the club toward the pair and the dead cur. Ellis bent down and said to Fowler, "They'll take care of you. I have to get after him." He then jumped up and began running in the same direction the animal-man had taken. As he ran, he took out his phone, pressed the recent recall button, and got Mo on the line.

"Mo, I'm after some guy that looks like a werewolf or something. Can you drive to the other end of the field behind the club and see if he comes out that way?"

"Can do, man. What do I do if he comes out?"

"Run over the bastard!"

Mo hadn't had this kind of excitement since he caught the last flight from Afghanistan. He turned his big sedan around, peeled out of the parking lot and headed for the far side of the field. Ellis continued his dash to where he saw the thing enter the waist-high crops. He knew it had too much of a head start for him to catch up immediately, but if it wasn't in as good a shape as he was, there was a high likelihood he might be able to run it down. That's what jogging three miles every morning will do for you, he told himself.

Reaching the edge of the mustard field, Ellis just started in when he almost tripped over something on the ground. He stopped, looked back and saw it was the elongated sleeve with the bear claws that the animal-man had been wearing. Realizing it might be potential evidence, he reached down and picked it up to take with him. *Damn, this thing is heavy*, Ellis said to himself. *Asshole much have shucked it so he could run faster.* The field was immense and clouds kept floating in front of the moon making it hard for Ellis to see what was in the distance. Every now and then he thought he saw his prey pop up, then dip down and take off again. Each time he did, Ellis would give chase. And each time he'd covered more ground, he'd find another piece of discarded wardrobe or weaponry to lighten the fleeing culprit's load. Good news, bad news Ellis knew. He was gathering lots of evidence, but his quarry was lengthening the distance between them.

When animal-man reached the far side of the field, Ellis was now burdened with armfuls of costume, uniform, war wear or whatever it might be called. The weight was causing him to huff and puff and struggle to stay in the chase. In the clearing ahead, he managed to see what was obviously the outline of a man now naked as the day he was born. Fatigued from the run, the man put his hands on his hips and begin walking to a large machine in the middle of a recently harvested onion field. Ellis couldn't yet determine what the strange machine in the field actually was. But he was positive he'd never reach the man in time if the thing was capable of movement.

Then an idea hit Ellis like a Smokin' Joe Frazier left hook. It was totally a shot in the dark, but at that moment, he didn't have any other shot to take. Dropping the animal paraphernalia to the ground, Ellis dug in his pocket, took out his phone, and called the number he had gotten only yesterday. It was picked up on the first ring.

"Howdy Pardner, Wild Bill here. Recognized the number you gave me."

"Bill, this is Ellis. Where are you?"

"Would you believe it? I'm back out at the FBO. Had an oil leak the guys found and called me about. So I came to take a look."

"Is the plane operational?"

"Damn straight. They fixed it up like nobody's business."

"Look, I'm really in a jam. Need you do something immediately, okay."

"What'd you have in mind, hoss?"

Ellis, who had continued moving as he talked on the phone,

could now see the full outline of the mysterious machine that had previously been only shadows. He now knew exactly what it was.

"Ever do any dog fighting in that plane of yours?"

"No. But not because I never wanted to."

"Well, how'd you like to take on a naked man in a helicopter?"

"*Wheweee*! You sure know how to entice a fellow, don't you?"

"It could get rowdy."

"Well, I would sure as hell hope so. Got a few more dollars to cover fuel cost?"

"Yes. But you have to move now."

"Give me the details, pilgrim. The Frontier Jew is ready for action."

CHAPTER 25

THE ROTORS ON THE CHOPPER had started to turn as Mo's Lincoln came barreling down a road bisecting the mustard and onion field. He had to hit the brakes hard to avoid slamming into Ellis who stepped from the field, trudged through the ditch, and then onto the shoulder of the road. Mo recognized him but had no idea what Ellis was cradling in both arms. It looked like a dead animal, maybe more than one.

Ellis flung open the back door, threw his burden on the floor board, then followed it saying, "He's in that onion field, let's go."

Mo dropped the gearshift of the four-door sedan into drive and stomped the accelerator. The big car swerved off the road, through the opposite ditch, and into the field. Even with the windows rolled up, the two could hear the whop-whop of the rotors as they roared toward it. Ellis told Mo, "Get beside it. Close enough for me to get a shot off."

"Don't think we're gonna get there before he takes off," Mo answered, just as the spin of the rotors began to swirl dirt into the air, throwing dust everywhere.

The sedan was still fifty yards away as the helicopter began to rise into the sky. The closer they got, the more the groundswell of debris kicked up by the chopper encircled them. There was little more they could do than try to look above it and see which way the craft was heading.

"What direction's he taking, Mo?"

"Appears to be headed south. Toward the outskirts, not the central city."

"Okay. Just follow as best you can until he's out of sight. I'm going to call it in."

"You got the cops on this already?"

"Not exactly," Ellis said. "But I do have a form of air support."

"No shit? You are one bad dude, man. But if you don't mind, put that gun back in your holster, okay? It's making me nervous."

"Done," Ellis responded, holstering the Glock and hitting recall on his phone.

"Wild Bill, you in the air yet?"

"Cruising like a swallow on the way to Capistrano. Which way to the target?"

"You need to head south of the central city. Then keep your eyes open for a three-rotor, two-seater, white Schweizer chopper. If you can find it, follow it. We just need to know where it goes, you don't actually have to engage."

"Come on, cowboy, where's the fun in that? Anyway, I'll shout if I see it, and you do the same. Right."

"10-4, Wild Bill."

"10-4… ha, I love this shit. Over and out, *jefe*."

"You got a guy in a helicopter looking for the other helicopter," Mo asked.

"Sort of. My guy's in a plane."

"Big ass plane?"

"Small plane. Big ass pilot."

"Oh yeah, what's his name?"

"Calls himself The Frontier Jew."

"Never heard of him."

"He's not famous, but he is enthusiastic. And right now, he's all we got going for us."

Wild Bill's plane was cruising smoothly but his imagination plus his internal antenna were in danger of redlining. As he swept south he scanned the skies for any trace of a rotary aircraft above, below, and to either side of him. For the first ten minutes he had the sky to himself, then fate dealt him a trump card. Fifteen miles beyond downtown, over an outdoor billboard encouraging drivers to take the next exit for Home Cooking At Cracker Barrel, he spotted a small white helicopter banking left. Wild Bill immediately went into pursuit mode. He dove hard to get a closer look at the aircraft and came perilously close to not being able to pull the nose of his plane up in time. But that ill-conceived and ineptly executed maneuver only heightened his sense of adventure as he leveled out and kept the chopper directly in front of him.

The Frontier Jew couldn't be certain that the naked helicopter pilot had somehow spotted the fixed-wing on his tail. But he must have. Else why would he start a series of radical aerial maneuvers that looked as if he was in the middle of an escape and evasion course. First the chopper banked hard right. Wild Bill followed suit. Then the whirly bird swung left. The fixed-wing did the same. Almost immediately, the helicopter went into a hard vertical climb. Eisenstat trailed like a shadow until he realized he was in danger of stalling at the top of his ascent. Fear momentarily wrapped a vise-like grip around him as he envisioned rolling over or tilting forward with too much momentum and starting a spin or nose-dive he'd never be able to pull out of. With his heart in his mouth, Wild Bill let the plane decelerate on its own and just as it was tipping forward he applied enough thrust to hopefully level out safely. While hope is never a preferred strategy, this time it proved consequential. Control of the plane was regained. Wild Bill had saved his ass, but lost the chopper.

It had been a half hour since Ellis's last contact with The Frontier Jew. The P.I. was fearful the killer had escaped him again. Behind the wheel, still heading south on Interstate 285, Mo was exceeding the speed limit even though neither he nor his passenger really had any idea where they were going. Then Ellis's phone rang.

"Hello."

"It's me, *compadre.*"

"Wild Bill… have you spotted him?"

"Tagged him. Chased him. Lost him. Then found the little bastard again."

"Which way… or where is he going?"

"Nowhere at the moment. Just sitting in his craft at the far end of a big parking lot outside a La Quinta."

"Does he know you're there?"

"Don't think so. I'm circling overhead but I'm pretty high. No place for me to set down nearby."

"Any idea of an address or street names?"

"Not sure, but a lot of the signage around here says Sandy Springs."

"Hold one second," Ellis said, then turning to Mo he asked, "La Quinta in Sandy Springs. Know where it is?"

"Know where Sandy Springs is. I can get the La Quinta coordinates on my Garmin. We're on the way."

Ellis quickly got back on with Eisenstat. "We're coming over now. Got enough fuel to keep circling?"

"Good to go, hero. I'll keep an eye on him and shout if that little whirly gig takes off before you guys get here."

"You think he sat down because he had trouble or because he's staying there," Ellis asked.

"Didn't see anything that looked like trouble. And he hasn't left his craft yet. If he does have a room, he's probably ruminating on the best way to get to it, still being buck naked and all."

"That's right," Ellis said to himself as well as Eisenstat. "Wait a second, let me check something." Putting his phone on the seat beside him, Ellis reached down in the floorboard brushing the furry sleeve and head dress aside. He retrieved the heavy buckskin jumpsuit that had been at the bottom. Turning it from one side to the other, he found the pockets and reached inside one. Nothing. Reaching in the second pocket, he felt something before he saw it and instinctively knew what it was. "Bingo," Ellis said to Mo, Eisenstat, and himself. Then he removed his hand and confirmed what he was holding. It was an electronic card for opening hotel room doors, still in the paper sleeve that clerks give to their guests, with the number 201 handwritten on the outside… right beside the La Quinta logo.

"If he goes in the hotel, we've got his ass," Ellis said into the phone.

"Well, it appears he's going in," Eisenstat responded. "Looks like he found a rag or something in the chopper. Not very big, but big enough for a do-it-yourself loin cloth. Of course, his ass and all the rest of him is still on display. Hope he corrals the same person who checked him in or he's liable to have trouble confirming his identity and getting back in his room."

"Hell," Ellis said, "they'll probably let him in just to get the naked fool out of the lobby."

"Getting close, man. Should only be another five minutes or so," Mo told Ellis.

"ETA in five," Ellis passed on to his eye in the sky. "Keep that chopper in your sight line."

"Affirmative, *Generalisimo*," Wild Bill responded. "If it moves, I'll move… and I'll shout while I'm doing it."

"Be safe," Ellis said into the phone.

"Better than sorry, your highness," The Frontier Jew responded. "Over and out."

CHAPTER 26

THE BIG LINCOLN PULLED INTO the main entrance of the Sandy Springs La Quinta. Then it slowly took a turn around the building. Ellis spotted the helicopter at the very back corner. Mo drove over to it slowly. Ellis got out of the car with phone in hand and looked up at the sky.

"Wild Bill, you still up there?"

"Yep. That you standing beside the whirley?"

"Affirmative. Haven't seen him come out of the building, have you?"

"Nope. They must have let him back in his room."

"Right. Listen, I'll take it from here. Why don't you go back to the FBO and park that plane. I'll call you and let you know where we should meet tomorrow."

"Sounds like a plan, man. Sure you don't need me to hang around?"

"No. I got it. Get some rest. And thanks for all your help. We'll figure out tomorrow what it cost me."

"That we will, lad, that we will. This is The Frontier Jew signing off… *sayōnara*, superstar!"

Ellis, still watching the sky, saw the Cirrus break its circular pattern and head east. Then he stepped to the open driver's side window of the car.

"Mo, need you to stay in the lot while I go in. Park nearby, someplace you can keep your eyes on the chopper, but not right beside it. If everything goes my way, I'll be escorting him out the back door and over to you in the next twenty minutes."

"What if everything doesn't go your way?"

"If you don't hear from me within the next half hour… either by phone or in person… take off. And all this animal crap in the floorboard, drop it at a police station. There's probably DNA all over it. Then call this number I'm about to give you. Ask for Lieutenant Carlyle. She won't be able to help right away, but hopefully, she'll be able to eventually follow up on it." Ellis wrote the phone number of the Phoenix hospital on the paper sleeve holding the key car. He kept the card and gave the sleeve to Mo.

"Hey, I can go in with you, man. I'm up for it," Mo volunteered.

"Appreciate the thought, Ellis said, "but I need you here in case he does come out alone. Someone will need to let the authorities know a killer is still on the loose."

"Still got bullets in that gun," Mo asked.

"Plenty," Ellis answered.

"Guess I don't have to tell you to make it snappy, then, huh?"

Somewhere, deep within the mind's phenomenal, but often mystifying resources, a bell rang within Ellis's head. "What did you just say?"

"Just want you to hurry, man. I don't want anything to go wrong up there."

"No… I mean, what did you just say exactly… about making it snappy?"

"I don't know. Something like… guess I don't have to tell you to make it snappy."

"Yeah, that was it." The phrase. The helicopter. Going into a potentially dangerous situation. His brain's internal storage was definitely trying to tell him something. But he didn't have time to figure it out.

Mo asked, "What is it, man?"

"Oh, nothing… I guess. Remember, if I'm not back in thirty minutes…"

"I take off. I got it. You be careful, man."

"Number one on my agenda," Ellis said. Then he turned and headed for the hotel, unaware of the fact that the man in room 201… the man who had just taken a shower and now had only a towel wrapped around him… the man who had walked to the window and saw Ellis and the cab by his helicopter… the man in the process of attaching a sedative projectile to his Pneu-Dart rifle… had returned to the window in time to see Ellis enter the back door of the hotel.

CHAPTER 27

ELLIS TOOK THE STAIRS RATHER than the elevator to the second floor. If his prey happened to be coming out as he was going in, he didn't want potential bystanders in harm's way. Entering the floor at the end of a long hallway, he looked at the room number on the first door he saw. It was 229. The other side of the hallway, 228. Now he knew which side he wanted, but it was at the far end of the building. Ellis walked slowly down the carpeted hall, keeping his hand ready to draw his weapon. He didn't want to expose it before it was necessary out of concern that potential guests might go batshit crazy seeing a man walking on their floor with a gun in his hand. If they raised a ruckus, it could alert the man he was after that something was amiss.

His walk was completed alone. No one came out of the elevator or any of the guest rooms. He was now outside room 201, staring at the door hanger reading "Do Not Disturb." Ellis put his ear to the door trying to listen for any sounds. He heard no television or radio, no music or conversation. There was almost silence, but not quite. He thought he heard the sound of water running. Not loud enough for a shower, perhaps the faucet in the bathroom. Maybe he was catching a break. Ellis removed his weapon from its holster with his right hand. With his left, he inserted the key card as silently, as he could. A little dot flashed green on the lock. Cautiously, Ellis pulled the door handle down, trying to make no sound at all. He succeeded. Then he began to slowly push the door open. Looking up and peering through the crack between the door and the frame, he could see the light from the bathroom but not inside it. The sound from the running water in the faucet was louder now. Continuing to push the door open gingerly, something compelled Ellis to look down. When he did, he saw that the carpet on the other side of the door was wet. Too wet. Son of a bitch! He was being set up. With no time to ponder whether his decision was right or wrong, Ellis put his shoulder against the door and slammed into it. The force rammed the man standing behind it into the wall. Ellis used all his strength and kept the pressure on, squeezing the man so tightly that he couldn't move his arms or legs, or the weapon now mashed against his chest and the door.

"Drop whatever you're holding," Ellis barked. "Or I'll put a round through this door and into your gut."

"I can't drop it, asshole," the man managed to reply. "You got me squeezed in."

Ellis believed him, but wasn't completely sure what to do next. If he released the pressure enough for the man to move his arms, it might enable him to swing his weapon around and get off a shot. So he paused momentarily with his feet bracing the opposite wall and his back pressed firmly against the door. *It may not be the best idea*, Ellis said to himself, *but at the moment, I haven't got a better one.*

"Listen," Ellis began, as he reached in his outside-jacket-pocket and retrieved a custom silencer made specifically to fit his Glock. Screwing it on, he said, "You're either going to find a way to get your hands off your weapon, or I'm going to shoot off your big toe that's sticking just under the edge of the door."

"What good will that do, you fuck? If I can't move, I can't move!"

"Well, you see, one, I bet you really can tear your hands away from that weapon even if you have to skin a few knuckles doing so. And two… it will just give me immense pleasure seeing your toe blown all to hell."

"You wouldn't do that, you—"

"THUMP!" Ellis put a round in the carpet just beside the man's toe. It burned, smoked, and smelled immediately.

"Okay, okay. I'll try, all right? I'll try."

Ellis could hear the sound of the man's hands scraping between the door on one side and the rifle on the other.

"Shit! This hurts man. Let up a bit on that door, will you?"

"No, I won't. And believe me, a few swollen knuckles is no pain at all compared to your toe exploding."

"Don't do that, man. I'll get it. I'll get it."

Ellis listened as more cursing was followed by more scraping of skin and metal. Then the man behind the door blew out a big breath. "Okay, they're free. I'm not holding the gun anymore."

"Tap on the door with your fingers. So I'll know where your hands are."

The man could move his fingers just enough for Ellis to place their sound somewhere below the man's waist and beyond the reach of his weapon. Using one foot to continue bracing himself, he moved his other leg so he could jump to his feet the minute he took pressure off the door. Not wanting the man to know when it was coming, he started a sentence he didn't intend to finish. "Here's the thing…" Then he jerked away from the door, sprung to his feet, and yanked the door toward him. Immediately, the man's rifle fell to the floor, along with the towel that had been covering his manhood.

For the slightest moment, Ellis was stunned. He was staring at a face he knew he had seen before, but he couldn't place it. The sedative rifle the man had been holding was now on the floor. Ellis knew if he reached down to pick it up, he'd be giving the man a chance to jump him, and he was in no hurry to provide that opportunity. It was definitely time to disable the guy. Without saying a word, Ellis drew his right foot back, then swiftly and with commitment, swung his leg forward and kicked the man squarely where incapacitation was sure to follow.

When a naked man gets kicked in the balls, he stays kicked. But he tends to do so off his feet, on his knees, moaning before he falls to the floor cradling his abused testes, and occasionally to top things off, he vomits. Ellis was hoping for three out of four, being not in the mood for the smell of the latter. He got his wish as the man simply lay on the floor writhing and twisted himself into something resembling a fetal position.

Now that his opponent was no longer a physical threat, Ellis looked around the room for something to keep him that way. There was nothing he could see that might be used to tie the man, but there was some sort of foot locker in the corner of the room. Ellis assumed it was what he had stored all his animal weapons and costuming in. Perhaps there was something in there he could use. Stepping over the moaning man and raising the top of the locker, he saw nothing to tie him with, but he did see a briefcase inside. Ellis reached in, grabbed the handle and tossed the case on the bed. He then thumbed the tabs sideways. The snaps popped open. Inside, there was nothing to tie the man with… but there was cash. Lots and lots of cash.

Questions began bouncing around Ellis's head like a jar of marbles spilled on a granite tabletop. Who was this guy?

He knew he had seen him somewhere but just couldn't place him. Where did all the money come from? Why had he been dressing like a werewolf and killing the people he'd been killing in such a vicious way? And why had he tried to make it look like Ellis had done it all? Way too many questions for a La Quinta hotel room in an Atlanta suburb. Need to move the guy to a different locale, Ellis determined. Some place where yelling and screaming and the causes of it wouldn't necessarily cause alarm from others close by. Ellis thought of just the place. Then he realized the man would have to be moved out of the room, down the stairs (or perhaps the elevator), through the main floor, and out the door. All without putting up a sizable fuss about being kidnapped. How to do that, Ellis pondered. But only for a moment. Once he remembered the man's sedative rifle was still lying on the floor, the rest of the plan came to him.

Ellis pulled the phone out of his pocket and called Mo.

The cabbie recognized the number immediately. "You okay dude? It's coming up on twenty-three minutes."

"I'm fine, Mo. But I need you to come up here. Room 201."

"Should I get the Smith and Wesson out of my glove compartment?"

"No need. By the time you arrive, our friend will be sound asleep. We've just got a little packing to do. Then we'll hit the road."

"Oh, yeah? Where we going?"

"Back to Bodacious."

CHAPTER 28

STUFFING A FIVE-FOOT, EIGHT-INCH MAN into a regulation military foot locker proved difficult but not impossible. Everything else had been removed. The die cut grips on either side provided a way for Mo and Ellis to tote the carrier, as well as a way for the occupant to get air should he regain consciousness. Even though it was heavy and burdensome, they decided to take it down the stairs and out the back door rather than lumbering through the lobby with it. Once it was hoisted into the trunk of Mo's Lincoln, Ellis went back to the room, retrieved the rifle and the briefcase, and left via the same route they'd taken previously. He thought about attempting to get the man's name from the desk clerk. A credit card was probably required when he checked in. Ellis assumed however, like most legitimate hotels, there was surely a policy against giving out names or room numbers. With the money he still had left and the securing of the briefcase, he had infinitely more than enough to bribe whoever was on duty, but since he had managed to abscond with both the man and the money without being seen by hotel personnel, he decided not to push his luck. Then a funny thing happened.

On his way to join Mo in the car, for some inexplicable reason, Ellis looked over at the helicopter still in the far corner of the parking lot. When he did, one of the eighty-six billion neurons in his brain spiked, releasing hundreds of chemical neurotransmitters that instantaneously enabled him to actually retrieve sensory information that once encoded, had been locked away in his mind's infinite storage vault. All of a sudden, and without warning, it all came together—the face of the man in the foot locker, the shape of the chopper on the ground—the mission he had always done his best to forget—it all came back to him. Though the presence of the man in this place, at this time, seemed virtually impossible, Ellis now knew who the man was.

When they arrived at Bodacious, Ellis told Mo to wait while he went inside. At the bar, he told Indigo he needed to see Fowler. She called as before and once again Maurice came out and escorted Ellis to Fowler's office. The club owner was seated behind his desk with an open bottle of Maker's Mark Bourbon and a half full tumbler in front of him. A T-shirt covered his torso and his left arm was wrapped in bandages from his shoulder to his wrist.

"Are you okay?" Ellis asked.

"Do I look okay?" Fowler answered.

"You've looked better."

"Did you kill the dog?"

"Yes."

"Why didn't you shoot him sooner?"

"I was afraid I might miss and hit you."

"Feel like I've been chewed on by a damn shark or something."

"Got something with me that might make you feel better."

"What's that?"

"The monster that sicked that dog-shark on you?"

"Really," Fowler said, taking a pull from his glass of whiskey and beginning a smile. "I'm starting to feel better already."

Ellis asked, "Got a quiet place I can talk to him without being disturbed?"

"Where is the bastard?"

"He's outside in the trunk of Mo's Lincoln."

Turning to his henchman, Fowler said, "Maurice, help Mr. Ellis recover his acquaintance, and take them to the storage room. Call me when it's set up."

Ten minutes later, Mo, Maurice, Ellis and the naked man were in the storage room that Ellis assumed was occasionally used for more than storage. He came to that conclusion based on the fact that as soon as Maurice turned on the lights in the room, he immediately retrieved a straight-back wooden chair from the corner, along with two lengths of rope from a shelf, plus a roll of duct tape from a desk drawer. When they opened the footlocker, the naked man was still drowsy from the carfentanil cocktail Ellis had shot into his ass. Maurice had no trouble putting him in the chair then tying his arms behind him and his feet together. "I'll call the boss," the behemoth said.

When Fowler entered the storage room and looked at the man in the chair, he said, "I've seen this guy. I know I have. But I can't remember where."

Ellis spoke. "Ex-Private Fowler, meet ex-Warrant Officer Henderson. The bird pilot who took us into our last mission."

The recognition was immediate. "Yeah, that's who it is. We saw him while we were waiting for you to get in. But then… wait a minute… you said you saw the chopper blown all to hell."

"I did," Ellis answered. "There was no doubt about it. And no one could have survived that missile strike… no one who was there. I simply made the assumption he was in the bird. He wasn't."

"Why the hell not?" Fowler asked, followed quickly by, "Where was he? And what's he been doing knocking off our old squad?"

"That's what we're here to find out," Ellis said.

Henderson, indeed, had a lot to answer for. But that had been the case for the majority of his life.

CHAPTER 29

EVAN THEODORE HENDERSON GREW UP feeling he had three strikes against him before he ever got to the plate. He was constantly teased and harassed by other kids simply because of his name. "Evan isn't even a name," they would say. Or "Theodore… oh, *T h e o d o r e*," they would mockingly elongate. Or they'd just go straight for the initials and chant, ET… ET… you even look like an extraterrestrial… an extra ugly one!" Which, to some degree, had a basis in fact. Evan was not a comely child. His teeth were crooked and his parents didn't have the money to fix them. His ears stuck out on the sides of his head like extended mirrors on the cab of an eighteen-wheeler. His nose was hooked and looked like it had started, flattened out, dropped off a cliff, and fell to a point just below virtually non-existent lips. As he grew, he had few friends, no real pals, and absolutely zero girls. The pretty ones didn't want to be seen with him. Even the plain ones who actually took pity on him preferred to do so at a distance. That was because Henderson's demeanor, behavior, and overall attitude were as unappealing as his looks.

He knew he was ugly so he didn't try to counter it by taking pride in his appearance. Often the clothes he wore looked as bedraggled as he did. He was standoffish around other people. When pressed by others to do something he didn't want to do, he'd become defensive, argumentative, frequently belligerent. His inability to let kidding and insults slide off his back, often led to physical altercations in which he seldom prevailed, leaving him even more ostracized and alone than he had been initially.

If one can actually become a hermit at an early age, Henderson did. He shunned human friends for those of the animal kingdom. Dogs, cats, birds, reptiles and the like, they all substituted for people who gave him a hard time. And often he took out his loathing of humans on the animals who showed no malice toward him. They became undeserving punching bags and far worse.

While a teenager, Henderson developed an interest in things both technical and regimented. He graduated from tearing the wings off dragonflies to memorizing the wing spans of aircraft. He stopped being mesmerized by the long straight lines of marching ants he'd step on and started being fascinated with the intricate formations and choreography of close order drill.

It was no surprise then, to his parents or himself, when he decided to join the army. The military could give him the technical expertise he wanted, with the discipline and organization he needed, all without the burden of striving to fit in. The army offered a life where one was accepted regardless of physical attractiveness or social acumen. Everyone wore the same clothes, stayed on the same schedule, followed the same orders. This was a life where the only thing that really mattered was proficiency. Henderson's grew exponentially, unfortunately in direct proportion to his alienation. And while various instructors recognized his apparently natural skills as a helicopter pilot, one individual uncovered and put to use Henderson's seemingly innate capacity for both cruelty and lack of remorse.

For some people, love is the ultimate motivator. It makes people do things they ordinarily wouldn't do, or know they shouldn't do. For other people—people for whom love has never really been a big part of their life—fear can be equally motivating. And a naked man strapped to a chair can be made to feel particularly fearful. Especially if he's just come out of a drug-induced stupor. So, after a few seconds of whispering to one another out of Henderson's earshot, Ellis and Fowler each approached him as Maurice and Mo stood against the wall.

Ellis spoke first. "Henderson, you are a loathsome degenerate. A cowardly murderer. There's no point in denying you've killed at least five people we know of, and tried to kill two others."

"I didn't do it," the bound man quickly said. "It was the dog. The dog killed 'em. I just messed 'em up a bit after they were already dead."

"That's what's known as a distinction without a difference," Ellis said. "Not that I necessarily believe you. But even if I do, you're still responsible, and you'll still have to pay."

"I got money," he spit out. "I can pay."

"That's not the kind of payment I'm talking about," Ellis said. "The facts are, you're either going to die right here, in a particularly long and painful way, or I'm going to take you back to New Mexico where you'll be arrested, tried, convicted, but unfortunately not executed. They no longer have the death penalty in that state."

"I'll take New Mexico," Henderson answered without being asked.

"Not that easy," Ellis replied. "First, you have to tell me what you know about the mission. The one you took us on and were supposed to take us out of. Then, you're going to have to explain what all this killing has been about… and why you were so determined to make it look like I was responsible."

"Look," Henderson began, "You got me. You got my stuff. You shot my dog. I'll cop to the killings when we get to New Mexico. I swear it."

Fowler had heard enough. He stepped between Ellis and Henderson. "You see this arm, asshole? Yeah, the one with all the bandages. Hurts like hell. But it's nothing compared to how you're gonna hurt unless you come clean. Want a taste of that? Want just a tiny taste of what it's going to be like?"

Fowler didn't wait for an answer. With his good hand, he reached in his jacket, pulled a silver Zippo cigarette lighter from his pocket and flipped it open, exposing the flame. "In addition to being an ugly fucker, you're kind of a hairy guy, aren't you? Don't seem to do a lot of manscaping, do you? Here, let me help." Then Fowler quickly reached out and set Henderson's pubic hair on fire.

Crackle, sizzle, and smoke preceded the bound man's scream, but only by a millisecond.

"Ahhhhh. Put it out! Put it out!"

Ellis grabbed a half empty beer bottle sitting on a counter. He stepped forward and doused the smoldering remains. "You get the idea, now? You see how this could go?"

Henderson was squirming, aching, crying, and pleading simultaneously. "I'll talk, okay. I'll talk. But just to you, okay. Not them. Not him. Don't let him near me, okay?"

"I'm sure my friends wouldn't mind stepping outside for the moment," Ellis replied. "But if I have to call them back in here…"

"You won't, I swear. I'll tell you what you want to know. I swear."

Ellis looked over at Fowler and nodded. The club-owner

turned to Maurice and Mo and said, "Let's step out for a few, fellas. I'm in need of a cigarette. And Mr. Henderson doesn't seem to care for the adverse effects of second-hand smoke."

The three walked out the door and shut it behind them. Ellis watched them go then turned to Henderson. "Now," he said, "I'm going to ask you a series of questions… which, by the way, we're going to record for posterity. But first," he continued, adjusting the picture on his smart phone so that only a close-up of Henderson's face was visible, "I need to make sure you're in focus. Oh, and by the way, if I get the slightest inclination that you're lying… Mr. Fowler, the gentleman with the lighter, will conduct the rest of your debrief."

CHAPTER 30

EARLY THE NEXT MORNING, ARRANGEMENTS agreed to the night before were already in motion. Ellis and Henderson were in the back of Mo's Lincoln on the way to the FBO. There, for a negotiated, and relatively exorbitant price, The Frontier Jew would meet them and fly the P.I. and his prisoner back to Arizona. The Grand Canyon State, instead of New Mexico, had been chosen by Ellis, over the protestations of Henderson, because it recently reinstated the death penalty. If Carlyle's condition were to reverse, and something terrible was to happen to her, Ellis wanted to make sure the man responsible for her injuries would suffer the full measure for his heinous act. If she did pull through, Ellis felt sure she'd want to be involved with the killer's extradition to Santa Fe where he'd have to stand trial for the grisly murders of Bevel and her ex-husband.

Ellis had been able to talk Fowler into going along with his plan by splitting the proceeds of Henderson's cash-laden briefcase. The club owner had initially wanted to snuff the bastard. Ellis had no qualms about using cash provided by ruthless people for the purpose of killing innocent people to make sure the murderer met his just reward. Of course, Fowler felt that a seventy-thirty split of the stash was more appropriate than fifty-fifty, since he was an actual victim of

Henderson's odious but now deceased pit bull. Ellis was able to persuade Fowler to settle for half when he advised that the club owner could greatly increase his compensation by simply sending a crew to Sandy Springs and quickly confiscating Henderson's helicopter. The Black man rather liked the idea of his own personal whirly bird so he accepted a half and half split of the cash with Ellis's commitment to never mention any knowledge of what could have possibly happened to the rotary aircraft. Such is the way deals are often made by those with differing agendas.

When Mo's Lincoln pulled up to the FBO gate, Ellis gave the attendant his name and he was directed to Hanger C. There, before he got out of the car, he reached over and gave Mo ten one-hundred dollar bills.

"Whoa… Mr. Ellis, this is really too much, man."

"No, it's not," Ellis replied. "Wish it could be more, but it's costing me a lot to get this guy back and there will be additional expenses after that. Not sure how much. But you definitely deserve the grand for helping me the way you have."

"Want any help getting him on the plane?"

"No, the pilot will lend a hand. He's certainly getting enough to do so."

Ellis opened the door, got out of the backseat, and helped Henderson, whose ankles had been tied with just enough rope to allow him to shuffle. His hands were tied also, tightly behind his back, and a strategically placed piece of duct tape kept him relatively silent.

Mo stuck his head out the driver's side window and said, "Well, guess I'll be going then. Next time you get to Atlanta, I hope you'll give me a call."

"Wouldn't want to ride with anyone else," Ellis said. "Good-by, Mo. Take it easy."

"You know me, Mr. Ellis, I take it any way I can get it." Then he punched the accelerator and took off to find his next fare.

Eisenstat, who was finishing his second double espresso, saw Ellis and Henderson coming. He couldn't help himself. "So, this is the flying animal-man, huh? Looks even less interesting with clothes on. Might have gotten some that fit."

"Didn't have time," Ellis responded. "Maurice was even hesitant to give up these. Called the sweat shirt and pants his favorite couch potato wear."

"Who's Maurice?"

"Obviously, a rather large fellow. Beyond that you don't need to know."

"That's what I like about you… closed-mouth and proud of it. Not like some, who just can't seem to stop talk—"

Ellis knew if he didn't cut him off they'd be there all morning. "Is the operator here going to give us any grief about this guy's restraints?"

"Nah… took care of that," Wild Bill said. "Told him you were a U.S. Marshall and that we were transporting a prisoner."

"He bought it?"

"No. But he agreed to look the other way for an extra two hundred. "I'll add it to you bill."

"How kind of you," Ellis snidely responded.

"All in a day's work, warrior. But let's not stand around gabbing with this guy looking like Anthony Hopkins' stand-in from 'Silence Of The Lambs.' Time to load and leave."

After hiking Henderson's arms higher up behind his back and hooking the rope round his hands over a nail in the wall, the pair hoisted the footlocker with the costume and weapons that were now effectively evidence, and stowed it behind the back seat. Henderson was unhooked next and shoved into one of the two back seats where the shoulder belt provided even more confinement. Twenty minutes after Ellis and Henderson had arrived at the FBO they were airborne.

Long flights affect different people in different ways. Ellis was content to put his head back and try to catch up on shut-eye he had gotten very little of over the last couple of days. Wild Bill was more than happy to regale their prisoner with episodes from what he thought of as his long and storied career as bon vivant, raconteur, and adventurer. Henderson, however, had more on his mind than listening subserviently.

The nail they had affixed Henderson to when they loaded the footlocker had managed to ever so slightly cut and fray the rope round his hands. Were they the hands of a normal man, the minor slit in the rope would have been of no consequence. But, as previous events had shown, Henderson was far from normal. With his hands behind him, and therefore unseen by his escorts, the animal-man had begun twisting and turning and tugging and pulling, and rubbing continually since being planted in his seat. The skin around his writs was rubbed so raw it had begun to bleed. A lesser man, a man to whom pain was a deterrent, would have given up long ago. But Henderson found the searing pain in his hands motivational. It convinced him he was making progress. It enticed him to believe that if he just kept at it, either the rope itself would break, or his bloody hands would become so slick that he'd be able to slide them loose. After hours of work, his damaged hands slid free. He would spend an additional half hour bleeding and plotting his next move.

"Mey. My man't mreathe."

Eisenstat, perturbed at having his monologue interrupted, said. "What's that? What did you say?"

Henderson repeated himself with more vigor. *"My man't mreathe! My man't mreathe!"*

Wild Bill reached over and shook Ellis awake. "I think he's saying I can't breathe. Perhaps he has a cold or something."

"*Mes! My man't mreathe!*"

"Okay, okay," Ellis said. Then he unsnapped his shoulder belt so that he could turn in his seat, reach back, and pull the tape from Henderson's mouth.

"If you become annoying, it goes back on," Ellis said. Then he flipped back around, refastened his shoulder belt, and hoped to go back to sleep. He wouldn't get the chance.

The animal-man pulled his arms from behind him and rapidly unsnapped his shoulder harness. Then he took the long piece of freed rope in each hand and flipped the bloody loop over the top of the seat in front of him, yanking it tight around Ellis's neck.

"What the hell—" was all Eisenstat could get out before Henderson yelled.

"Set this plane down! Set it down now or I'm gonna garrote the sonofabitch!"

Ellis was trying with all his might to get his fingers between the rope and his throat. He couldn't do it. He brought one hand down and tried to unsnap the belt holding him in place but he was thrashing about too much to locate the release. As his throat constricted more and more, his legs started kicking out in front of him as his face became redder and redder.

Eisenstat immediately punched in his fully digital three-axis auto pilot. The plane leveled out. He released his harness and reached under his seat. When he found what he wanted, he turned in his seat and pointed his forty-five caliber Colt Bluntline Special at Henderson's head.

Wild Bill shouted, "Release him now! Or it's *adios, amigo.*"

A cautious man would have considered his options. A reasonable man would have weighed the alternatives. A sane man would have done as he was told. Henderson, being none of the aforementioned, gripped the rope round Ellis's neck even tighter with his right hand and grabbed the twelve inch barrel of the firearm with his left. Then, for reasons known only to himself, the animal-man started screaming at the top of his lungs. *"Ahhhhhhh! Ahhhhhhh! Ahh—"*

As the piercing screeches reverberated around the cabin, Ellis continued to thrash,

Eisenstat added a second hand to hold onto the weapon that Henderson was doing his best to dislodge, and the Cirrus continued to float through the clouds like a hawk on an updraft.

For what it was worth—and it would prove to be expensive in the extreme—Henderson came to the conclusion that he'd have a decided advantage possessing the gun rather than the man he was choking. He let go of the rope with his right hand and moved it to the barrel as well. As Ellis struggled mightily to catch his breath, a world-class tug of war ensued between Henderson and Eisenstat. The animal-man had thrown his back against his own seat and raised his legs to push against the seat in front of him for maximum pulling power. The Frontier Jew was using his hands, his elbows, his forearms and the weight of his body against his seat to hold on for dear life. Ellis was simply trying to get enough air to keep from passing out.

In times such as these, the potential for unintended consequences increases exponentially.

Henderson—who had yet to stop screaming—had pulled the barrel to within an inch of his face. Eisenstat—who was about to be wrenched from the pilot's seat—decided to give one last great jerk to wrench the pistol from his foe's grasp. When he did, the restored (but apparently not perfectly so) antique firearm discharged.

Deafening is perhaps too mild a word, but it's the one that came to Ellis's mind when he saw fire spring from the barrel, followed closely by a good chunk of the animal-man's skull rocketing blood, brain matter, and the bullet itself into the back of the plush leather passenger seat.

Less than a second passed before Wild Bill said, "Thank God for luxury!" Might have been tricky if the slug pierced the fuselage."

"Why'd you shoot him?" Ellis yelled, his hearing yet to recalibrate after the blast.

Eisenstat answered just as loudly. "Hey, I never pulled the trigger. Damn thing just went off on its own."

"Jesus, what a mess," Ellis moaned, no longer feeling the need to shout.

"That's for sure," Eisenstat responded. "Have to charge a hell of a cleanup fee."

After their heartbeats returned to something approaching normal, both were quiet for the next hour or so. Ellis was methodically going over what they'd have to do next, who he'd need to explain things to, and how to get on to the next steps that somehow now were more important than ever. Eisenstat was mentally creating the first verbal draft of this new and outrageous exploit. He pictured himself delighting listeners with it for years to come.

Eventually, Ellis spoke.

"Say, you wouldn't happen to know a mortician and an *itamae* who might be a bit on the shady side… do you?"

The Frontier Jew quickly replied, "Hell, Ace, doesn't everyone?"

CHAPTER 31

THE REST OF THE RETURN journey to Arizona included an extended conversation regarding the arrival of a plane in Sedona with a dead body inside. Eisenstat indicated that after touching down, he could taxi directly to his rented private hanger. There, the two could perform an extensive cleaning of the Cirrus as well as an appropriate boxing of Henderson's body for whatever Ellis had in mind. Having agreed upon next steps, and with less than an hour to touchdown, Ellis took the opportunity to do a check-in on Carlyle.

"Hello. Nurse Meyers speaking."

"Hi, Flo. It's me. What's the latest on Lieutenant Carlyle?"

"Oh, hello. Yes, I recognize your voice. You can even give me your real name now if you like… or, let me guess. Is it Ellis. Brig Ellis?"

"Police been talking about me?"

"Not only the police, but Ms. Carlyle as well. She's really had a change for the better. The doctors have updated her condition from serious to stable, and they say that with rest and the appropriate amount of physical therapy, she can then move on to the plastic surgery."

"Therapy? Plastic surgery? You're way ahead of me, Flo."

"Oh, yes… I guess we never really got into specifics over the phone, did we? Well, you see, she came extremely close to losing her right arm. The doctors went back and forth about whether to amputate. But now it looks like with extensive physical therapy, she should be able to regain use. Or, at least, partial use. But it will take some time."

"And what about the plastic surgery?"

"Well, I'm afraid the right side of her face was terribly damaged. Bites. Claw marks. That sort of thing. Though, again, the doctors here believe the latest reconstruction techniques can mask a lot of the scarring."

Jesus, Ellis thought to himself. *A vibrant, striking young woman, nearly torn apart.* The impact of Meyers' words further cemented his resolve, and his involuntary pause gave the nurse the opportunity to keep talking.

"Oh, and you should know that she told the police you had nothing to do with her assault. She told them what you were doing when she was attacked, and that you couldn't have had anything to do with it."

"Flo, can she have visitors?"

"Yes. Absolutely."

"Tell her I'm coming, okay? Not sure of the exact timing, but it will be tonight or tomorrow. Let her know I'll be there, okay?"

"I certainly will. She'll be glad to see you, I know. I told her that we've talked on the phone and she had some very nice things to say. She thinks rather highly of you."

"And I, her. And, you too, Flo. Thanks for all you've been doing for her... and for me."

After saying good-bye to Nurse Meyers and turning his phone off, he turned to Eisenstat.

"After we land, clean up, and make arrangements for Henderson, I need to go to Phoenix."

"Want to fly?"

"No. I'll just rent a car and drive down. Don't have to worry about staying out of sight and off the grid now."

"You know," Eisenstat began, "those rental car companies can cost you an arm and a leg. Then there's the insurance thing you have to prove. Plus the hassle of finding a car on the lot and returning it when you get back, and—"

"Where are you going with this," Ellis asked, somehow already knowing the answer.

"Well, I could let you borrow my Range Rover and you wouldn't have to deal with all that red tape and whatnot."

"And you would do this out of the goodness of your heart?"

"No. I would do this for say… half of what the rental car company would charge."

Chuckling, Ellis said, "Is there anything you possess that doesn't have a red tag sale or a blue light special on it?"

The Frontier Jew needed no time to formulate an answer. He immediately responded, "My reputation, lad. The good name of Wild Bill Eisenstat. It is as they say… priceless."

CHAPTER 32

After arriving at the hospital in Phoenix, but prior to going up to the floor where Carlyle was recovering in a private room, Ellis stopped in the gift shop and purchased two different flower arrangements. Holding each in separate hands, he stopped at the nurses' station and asked if Meyers was in. The young candy striper, momentarily holding down the desk, told him that she'd be there in an hour and a half when the shift changed. Ellis said he'd like to leave the flowers for her—with a card that read: *Thanks for all your help.* The young woman assured him it would be given to Nurse Meyers upon her arrival. He then asked her for Lieutenant Carlyle's room number and she willingly obliged.

As Ellis approached the room, he noticed that a uniformed policewoman was stationed outside the door. He gave her his name and asked to enter. She told him to wait while she checked with the patient inside. Returning quickly, she told Ellis he could go in, but to leave the door open. He, somewhat begrudgingly, complied.

Ellis had already steeled himself against what he might see. He was determined not to show shock, and certainly not pity. It quickly became difficult for Ellis to keep either at bay. Carlyle was on her back, her head, particularly the right side, was covered in bandages with a small-diameter plastic tube running down to a drainage receptor. The right side of her body was bandaged heavily also, and virtually all of her right arm was in a cast. Ellis hoped outrageousness would mask his concern.

"Wow… do you look fucked-up!"

It quickly became apparent that while parts of Carlyle's body was seriously injured, her intellect and sense of humor had survived intact.

"Is that a medical term," she asked, sarcastically. "Should we record that on the chart?"

"Just an observation," Ellis said, trying to keep things as light as possible. "Though I get the feeling your hard-boiled attitude escaped injury."

"May look like that from where you're standing, but from my vantage point, it's been run over by a truck. Just don't let anyone know, okay?"

"Your secret's safe with me," Ellis replied, amazed at her capacity for banter after everything that had happened. "I won't imply to anyone that you've done anything other than rake me over the coals. And certainly, if they know you at all, they'll believe it."

"Tell me, Ellis, why do you look like you just stepped out of *GQ* and I look like the bride of Frankenstein?"

"That's a long story, Lieutenant. Sure you got the time?"

"Do I look like I'm going anywhere?"

"A Halloween Ball perhaps, but barring that, not really."

"You have my undivided attention, private investigator Ellis, unless of course I happen to doze off. The drugs they're pumping into me would be responsible for that. Don't view it as a sign you're more boring than usual."

"I'll take no affront then, and I'll bring you up to speed as best I can. Though, at a certain point we may want things to be a bit more private."

"Meaning you're going to make a pass at me in my defenseless position?"

"No. Meaning I may need to share information that, at this point, only you should hear. And I'll probably ask you to ask your sentry to keep the door closed for a bit."

"We can do that. But you have to understand that she's a romantic. She'll probably think you're really going to make a pass at me and that I want you to."

"You mean you don't?"

"Depends on how interesting your story is. I sometimes get excited listening to after-action reports."

"You might want to ask them to cut back on those drugs a bit."

"Later. For now, let's hear what you've been up to."

Ellis didn't exactly begin at the beginning. First, he made a point of thanking her for setting the record straight with all those who wanted to immediately pin previous murders and the attempt at her demise on him. Then he began to cover exactly what he'd been doing since coming to his senses in the middle of the Yavapai Apache reservation. When he got to the capture of Henderson, he said. "This is the part we might want to keep to ourselves."

"Ask the officer to come in," she said.

Ellis did so, and when she came in Carlyle said to her, "Officer, we need to go over some sensitive information about the case. Please keep the door closed for a bit if you don't mind."

The police woman looked at Carlyle, then Ellis, then a smirk crossed her lips. "Sure. No problem."

When she left, Carlyle said, "Told you what she'd think."

"Still able to read people, huh. That's a good sign."

"Let's get back to your report. You've nabbed the guy."

Ellis picked up where he left off, but he decided to leave a few details out. Like Fowler setting Henderson's pubic hair on fire. Then he was ready to show her Henderson's confession which he had recorded on his phone. When it began, she asked, "Why are you cropped in so tight? I mean a close-up is one thing, but…"

"Don't concern yourself with my directorial decisions. Just listen to what he has to say."

As she watched and listened, she became convinced of two things. One, the man was certifiably insane. And two, that didn't necessarily keep him from telling the truth. She believed his remarkable story.

"I take it you think he's telling the truth," she said to Ellis.

"I do. Do you?"

"Yes. I do. But I don't think he'll make a very good witness. The man's obviously demented. A good defense attorney will turn him and his story inside out on cross examination."

"Probably not," Ellis countered.

"Why's that?"

"Because he's dead."

"Dead? Damn. All right, give me the rest of it."

Ellis went on to detail what happened in the plane, neglecting specifics regarding Henderson's body, other than to say it had already been cremated… which, it actually hadn't been yet, but soon would be.

"You know," Carlyle began, "it's going to be very difficult, maybe impossible to actually prove what he said. I doubt there was any form of written or recorded communication between them. And since Henderson was the puppet involved with the actual wet work, the physical evidence you talked about won't be a link to the guy who was pulling the strings."

"You said you believed him."

"I do. But—"

"We both believe him," Ellis said. "But right now, you can't do anything about it. And like you said, it's unlikely the law will be able to either. On the other hand, I can."

"Now wait a minute, Ellis." She tried to sit up a bit, but it hurt too much to move. Moaning momentarily, she settled back down before she spoke. "I know you want to, but you can't take this personally."

"Oh really," he responded, incredulous at her remark. "I haven't shared with you the totality of what happened on that mission he discussed. I don't intend to. But the point is, their plan was to have us all die then and there. When that didn't happen, the whole thing was swept under the rug. And apparently put on a shelf to be taken down later whenever necessity called. Look, the best man I ever soldiered with was murdered. So were the other members of my squad. So were two people who had nothing to do with any of that. They were killed simply because it was now useful to make it look like I was the crazy one. And you… look what was done to you… all because you were involved with me. I take all of that pretty damn personal."

"What are you going to do?"

"You don't want to know."

"Another confession would help," she said. "As long as it doesn't look like it was only made under duress."

"Got a feeling duress is probably going to be called for."

"Tell me what you plan to do."

"If I don't tell you, you can say you didn't know. And you won't be lying."

"Whatever you're thinking, you should re-think it?"

"That would be overthink. Listen, if things go awry… or,

even if they don't, when you're back on your feet, there's a footlocker in an airplane hangar at the Sedona airport. The footlocker has all of Henderson's paraphernalia in it. I'm sure its covered with multiple DNA from multiple victims. I'll leave a copy of the phone recording with it. The hanger's rented by William Eisenstat. He'll confirm everything I've told you. I'll write his name on this notepad by your phone, in case you don't remember it."

"I am getting a bit drowsy. The drugs, you know."

"Yeah, drugs will do that."

"Should talk you out of whatever…"

"No you shouldn't. You should just rest. Get some sleep. It's good for you."

"…m sleepy. Can't help…"

"You don't have to help anything. I just wanted you to know that the bastard who did this to you has already paid for what he did. And the bastard who put him up to it… is going to."

CHAPTER 33

THE FLIGHT WAS CROWDED BUT Ellis didn't particularly mind. No longer having to operate in fugitive mode, and still in possession of most of Henderson's cash after his split with Fowler, the P.I. had booked a first class round trip ticket. He was sitting back, enjoying a complimentary glass of champagne, and thinking about the last couple of days plus the two or three that loomed before him.

True to his word, Eisenstat had introduced him to a couple of individuals who were skilled in their respective vocations and also amenable to coloring outside the lines if the price was right. Ellis again used his purloined cash to make sure it was, and soon the vast majority of Henderson's body underwent a fiery disposal. If anything approaching a soul or spirit remained, Ellis assumed it would get a similarly warm reception at the gates of hell. The itamae who had been selected plied his trade well and provided Ellis with exactly what he requested. He went on to suggest that if his handiwork wasn't going to be utilized right away, a device to keep everything temperature controlled would be recommended. Never one to skimp, particularly with someone else's ill-gotten gains, Ellis purchased a Yeti Hopper Flip insulated cooler bag with a shoulder strap for easy handling. It was stowed in the overhead compartment directly above him, as opposed to his Glock 19 with accompanying ammunition that the airline required be housed in a locked case and stowed away safely in the plane's baggage compartment.

As the Boeing 767 headed northeast and winged its way high above the states leading to Washington D.C.'s Ronald Reagan National Airport, Ellis tried to keep his mind on the task ahead of him rather than the recent sordid events that made his trip necessary. In the past, he had done whatever he could to keep bygone tragedies behind him, but one proved impossible. It always had, really. It was always there, silently in wait, the mission he couldn't forget and the men who were involved. Men who did their duty and more. Plus men, from his knowledge now, who had abdicated their roles as comrades and patriots for those of traitors and murderers. There was Henderson, of course, and there was one other. One whose last contact with Ellis came vividly back, with words that took on a totally different interpretation now.

"You and your snake eaters ready, Ellis?"

"Born ready, Sir."

"Bang-bangs?"

"Locked and loaded."

"Secret squirrel start to finish, son."

"Zero leaks, Colonel."

"Good. Concerns?"

"Rations? Meals RTE?

"This is in-and-out. Ammo only. Hot chow when you get back."

"Ten-four."

"Weather's not optimal, but Henderson handles a Black Hawk like his bassinet was a bucket seat."

"Any changes in the primary, Colonel?"

"Negative. Just bag bandits and bolt."

"Will do, Sir."

"Good hunting, lad."

When it was over, when the squad had emerged from The Empty Quarter and come back, Ellis's debrief had been perfunctory. He wasn't surprised. He had taken on a number of missions that were off the books, that as far as the Army was concerned, never happened. None had ever gone as wrong as this one did, but that's the luck of the draw, he thought. No one could particularly explain why their ride got disintegrated, or why a superior force had chased them as long as they did. Fortunes of war, it was chalked up to. Somehow the enemy got wind of their presence. Shit happens.

Of course, no one who was connected to that particular mission was still around. The chopper pilot, everyone assumed, was dead. The squad had lost one of its own and was quickly broken up and reassigned. The Colonel had been transferred and shipped out before the squad even got back. Bureaucracy at work, Ellis thought at the time. Now he knew better. *"Secret squirrel, start to finish, son,"* the Colonel had said. Then, Ellis took it simply as a secret mission that wouldn't be recorded for all the world to see. He now knew it was the Colonel's, and only the Colonel's personal project. *"In and out. Ammo only. Hot chow when you get back."* Ellis now knew it wasn't simply operation protocol, the Colonel had no intention of any of the squad ever coming back. *"Good hunting, lad."* Ellis had no idea then that he didn't really mean it. The P.I. doubted that his ex-commander would offer 'good hunting' now that the Colonel himself was the prey.

CHAPTER 34

THOUGH HE HAD BEEN OUT of the military for some time, Randolph Winslow Harrison still preferred to be addressed as Colonel. It added panache to his campaign for United States Senator, and encouraged people to think of him less as a politician and more as an ex-military man, warrior, protector of America both on and off the battlefield. His physical presence was part of the package. Tall, not thin but not overweight. Well-groomed salt and pepper hair that had begun to recede somewhat, but still more a positive than a negative. The Colonel took pride in how he looked. He was constantly cognizant of the image he projected to other people. Always had been. A son of the south from a wealthy clan, young Randolph was continually reminded that he was a reflection of the Harrison family and as such should always appear to be honest, brave, and of the highest moral character.

The problem was, in reality, he was none of the three. From a very young age he found it infinitely less troublesome to simply blame someone else for any mishaps that he was actually responsible for. He was delighted to find that people tended to believe his protestations of innocence and his feigned reluctance to name names. His act was a good one and always seemed to do the trick when necessary. Bravery was simply not threaded through his personal DNA, and he never seemed to find a way to develop it. He would never be the first to try something new or dangerous. He would however, pay close attention to those who did, enabling him to discuss precisely how he had overcome certain challenges that, in fact, had been overcome by someone other than himself. And when it came to high moral character, he developed a second sense for when it was necessary to seemingly take a position on principle. A position arrived at less by fealty to truth and fairness and more by recognition of what would be in his own best interest—assuming he could achieve the latter without exposing his disdain for the former.

The military had been a tradition in his family. Multiple generations of ancestors could boast, and often did, of service under fire from Khe Sanh to Inchon to Iwo Jima to Meuse Argonne, all the way back to Gettysburg. Those Harrisons generally volunteered for combat. The Colonel did everything he could to avoid it. When it appeared he'd be unable to do so however, he generally found ways to stay far behind the front lines, convincing his superiors that his talents for tactics and administration were of far greater value than simply of one more officer in the field.

Now, his ability to inflate his worth and convince others of his outstanding acumen was reaching its zenith as he enjoyed a five to eight point lead in virtually all the reputable polls. Randolph Winslow Harrison was on the cusp of becoming the next United States Senator from Virginia, and as his recent clandestine operations had shown, he was not going to let anything—present or past—stand in the way of that.

CHAPTER 35

THE BLACK AND WHITE TWO-STORY colonial was on an idyllic tree-lined street in Fairfax. It was the kind of home that looked perfect on the front of a flyer reading: *A Vote For Harrison Is A Vote For Virginia.* The home had actually belonged to Harrison's wife's family. She had been dead for the past two years, felled by a massive stroke that saw her drop dead in the middle of eating ice cream at the kitchen table. Even though it was a far larger home than one person needed, Harrison had seen fit to hold onto it due mostly to its appropriate stateliness.

Ellis had been watching the house two days and nights. He had parked his rental unobtrusively down the street, in different places each time. The last thing he wanted was to be made by any authorities that might be assigned to keep an eye on the candidate and his home. Ellis had binoculars and used them, but only when it was apparent that there was no one watching him. Recon, he knew, was as much about not being seen as seeing. That's why he wouldn't park in the same place twice, or leave his car parked where it was overnight. Once all the lights in Harrison's place were out for at least two hours, Ellis would abandon his stakeout, go back to his hotel, and get up early enough the next morning to be in position before anyone arrived at the Colonel's place, or before he left to go elsewhere.

Most people are addicted to routine. Taking the same route to work every day. Seeing guests to the door and bidding them goodbye either inside or out. Doing one's ablutions in the same order. The Colonel wasn't immune. Ellis observed that each night, all the lights on the first floor of the house would be put out, then a light would be turned on upstairs. Then, approximately five to eight minutes later, the light upstairs would go out, a few seconds would pass, and a light in a corner room on the first floor would come on. It would stay on anywhere from fifteen minutes to a half hour. Then it would go out, and no other lights would be turned on. Ellis surmised that the Colonel was turning off the house lights before retiring… going upstairs to prepare himself for bed… then returning to the room below for reading, a nightcap, or whatever. He decided to spend one additional night watching, just to be sure. When history repeated itself for the third time, he decided he'd go in the following night when the upstairs light went on. Doing so would enable him to be in place to greet the Colonel when he came back downstairs.

On the fourth night, Ellis came fully prepared. He wore all black, including gloves and a ski mask. He brought everything he needed. A DX40 nickel-plated pole identifier to temporarily magnetize the alarm system and render it inoperative. A Bogata rake insertion device to pick the back door lock. His smartphone that showed one confession and would hopefully record another. The cooler and its contents, to bring finality to all that had gone on. If all went as planned, no one other than the Colonel would know that he'd ever been there. And if it didn't go as planned, he also had his Glock with silencer plus a full clip.

The Colonel finished preparing himself for bed, then, as was his routine, trundled downstairs to the library for three fingers of twenty-one year old scotch prior to retiring. When he turned on the lights, he immediately saw Ellis sitting in a leather-tufted chair in front of his desk holding a pistol that was pointed his way. Initially startled, but not wanting to show fear, the Colonel segued immediately into outrage.

"Who? What the hell is this? Who are you," the Colonel barked with no time in between for actual answers to his questions.

"You don't recognize me, Colonel? I admit, it's been a number of years. But neither of us has changed that much."

"You… you're… that lieutenant. Lieutenant… Ellis, right?"

"Bingo. Nice of you to remember."

"What the hell are you doing… in my house… at this time of night… in that damn ninja getup? You can be charged with breaking and entering, you know. And you're brandishing a weapon. Hell, man, that's a felony offense. You're really asking for it."

"No," Ellis began. "I haven't really come to ask for anything. I've come to tell you a few things. Then I'll listen."

"And just what do you expect to be listening to?"

"I expect you're going to tell me why you sabotaged our mission and attempted to have us all killed while we were in-country. Of course, that didn't work out the way you planned it. But now, ten years later, you put a plan in place to knock us off one by one. Spoiler, Colonel, your plan came close, but there's no cigar. Now… you're going to come clean before either of us leaves this room tonight."

"You don't know what you're talking about. You must have PTSD or something like that. That's why you've broken into my home. It's why you're holding me at gunpoint. If people have been killed, for all I know, you probably did it."

"I know that's the story you wanted told, Colonel. But it

simply won't wash. Not now that I've got the goods on both Henderson and you."

"Who's Henderson? I don't know any Henderson. I don't know what you're talking about."

"You know, Colonel, I was more than willing to let you tell your story your way. To let you explain without… I think the term is duress… yes, to let you explain without duress your involvement in these savage murders. But I assure you… if duress is necessary… it will be applied."

A tiny crack began to snake its way into the Colonel's false bravado. Sweat appeared on his forehead and upper lip, and it wasn't hot in the room. What the hell's happened, he wondered. Why hadn't he heard from Henderson in the last few days? How much did this man holding a gun on him already know?

"Look, I told you once, I don't know anything about this Henderson or why you're here. I'm serious."

"I'm serious too, Colonel. Serious as a flat-lining heart attack. I'll prove it. Drop into that chair behind the desk. I want you to have a good look at what I've brought with me."

The Colonel, now sensing something had gone terribly wrong, did as he was told. At the moment, he saw no other alternative. Ellis put the phone on the desk. He tapped the icon that opened the recording. Then he said, "You're about to see an old friend of yours."

The playback began, and there was Henderson, looking wild-eyed and afraid and spilling his guts. The animal-man flipped on the Colonel like slow motion flapjacks in midair. He said the Colonel had come to him initially. Befriended him. Said he knew all about Henderson's personal history and his enjoyment of pursuits other people didn't have a taste for. He asked if Henderson would like to make some money. More money than he'd ever make on his own. All he had to do was take out a few ex-soldiers who the Colonel told him had been bad apples anyway. But he had to do it a certain way, and he had to make sure the killer's trail would lead to Ellis.

The animal-man's soliloquy didn't contain itself to simply planning and preparation; Henderson went on to describe in detail how he murdered five people, and attempted to murder two others. He pointed out that the Colonel had paid him half his murderous bounty in advance, and that the other half would be delivered once the mission was completed. He even detailed how the Colonel had arranged for Henderson to have the use of a helicopter so his tasks could be performed more quickly, as well as enabling him to stay ahead of his targets, or pursuers, if it came to that.

When Ellis tapped the phone and the recording stopped, the Colonel paused before speaking. When he did, his tone was less demanding, more defensive. "The man's obviously crazy. He's making it all up. You had him over a barrel, he needed to come up with answers. So he blamed the first person who came to mind."

"Why do you think you came to mind?"

"Well... because we were all part of the same mission, you know. Him. You. Me. He made the connection. He thought you'd be more likely to believe all that rot about someone you actually knew. That's why he implicated me. Yes. That must be why."

"If that's so, Colonel, then tell me why the briefcase with the money... the money you paid to Henderson, had your fingerprints all over it... as did the cash."

"What... what are you—?"

"After hearing what Henderson had to say, I had a friend of mine in the FBI test the whole thing for prints." Ellis wished he had done so, but he hadn't. It was a bald-faced lie, but the

Colonel had no way of knowing that. "The test was through both civilian and military records. Your prints came up. A ten-point match."

The Colonel sat stunned and silent. He didn't know what to say. Ellis realized his trick had worked. He kept the pressure on.

"You realize, of course, that if any of this gets out, the end of your quest to become a United States Senator will be disappointing I'm sure, but it will be nothing compared to the rest of your life behind prison walls or the death penalty via a needle in your arm. Sure, they say it's painless, but personally, I sort of doubt it… and why be the one to find out?"

Why? The Colonel's mind was racing. Ellis seemingly had him dead to rights with the Henderson confession and the finger prints. Why did he say, 'why be the one to find out'? Was he offering him a way out of this thing?

The Colonel spoke. "You asked, why be the one to find out? I mean, just for the sake of a hypothetical, does that mean I may not have to? Are you offering some kind of deal?"

Ellis looked him in the eye, and still kept the gun pointed at him as he said, "I'm not offering anything, Colonel. I'm telling you how things are going to be. Let's start with the fact that you're responsible for a hell of a lot of death. And you are going to be punished for that. But there's no law that says I shouldn't benefit from your punishment. You see, Colonel, you're not the only one who recognizes enlightened self-interest when he sees it. There's no reason I shouldn't get something out of this for everything I've been through. And I've determined how to do that."

Individuals who are avaricious, empathize with the trait in others. The Colonel was momentarily delighted to find it might be part of Ellis's makeup. "What did you have in mind," he asked.

CHAPTER 36

"I COULD KILL YOU FOR WHAT you've done. And I admit I'd get some measure of satisfaction from doing that. But I feel I'm due a lot more than satisfaction. So we're going to do two things. One… Henderson said you gave him half the money you promised up front, with the other half to be paid once the job was completed. You'll give that other half to me. You'll also give me a recorded confession, just like Henderson did. A confession that will be my insurance policy. You see, if something were to happen to me later on, a copy of that confession along with the fingerprint results would be automatically forwarded to the authorities, and you'd be… I believe the phrase is… shit out of luck."

"How do I know you aren't lying? How do I know that once I've recorded it you wouldn't use it against me?"

"Well, you can't be certain. But look at it from my point of view. As long as I have it and don't use it, I've got protection from payback, as well as having a United States Senator in my coat pocket. Who knows when that might come in handy?"

The Colonel had to admit it made perfect sense to him. Why would anyone give up wealth and power simply for retribution? Still, he was cautious. "What if I say no? What if I won't do it?"

"Then," Ellis began, "I'll simply stick the end of this Glock in your ear, and blow your megalomaniac brains all over the wall. I'll make sure there are powder burns on your hand and everyone will assume you took yourself out. Because I'll also type a note on your computer saying how you can no longer live with the evil that you've done. And... that you hope God, in his infinite and compassionate nature, can find a way to forgive you. Whoever finds it will surely put the wheels in motion to tell the world what a loathsome degenerate you actually were. Which of course, won't matter to you, because you'll be dead."

The Colonel was sweating profusely now, and hoping against hope that the potential life jacket he was apparently being thrown, wouldn't sink beneath the waves with him in it.

"The other half of the money I was going to give Henderson, and the confession, and that will be it. Right?"

"Right. My money. My insurance policy," Ellis responded.

The pause was somewhat less than pregnant. "All right. Turn that damn thing on."

Ellis told him to begin at the beginning and he did. The Colonel detailed that when they were in country, he had been assigned to Truce Talks with the American military delegation, high-ranking government officials from the combatant nations, as well as representatives of various tribal warlords who were now in charge of multiple swaths of occupied territory. He explained how he had been clandestinely approached by one such warlord's representative and offered a king's ransom to take out a cell of terrorists who had been playing one side against the other for the sake not of Allah's eternal gratitude and multiple ethereal virgins, but for enormously lucrative opium profits skimmed from ill-educated and unwitting bureaucrats. Yes, while peace was being negotiated, treachery was being planned. Treachery that would use Ellis's squad as pawns to wipe out the double-dealing terrorists and then be wiped out themselves so that no trace of the action could ever be walked back to it instigators. The motive was payback, the method was annihilation, and the momentum behind it all was greed. Some things are indeed eternal.

The Colonel went on to acknowledge that once Henderson dropped Ellis's team in, he didn't let his co-conspirators kill the chopper pilot as well because he thought one as manipulative as Henderson might prove useful in life after enlistment. That proved to be the case when the Colonel's senate aspirations made it necessary to eliminate any and all potential links to the abomination that had simply become known as the mission. Dead men indeed, tell no tales.

When the Colonel stopped talking, Ellis stopped recording.

"That enough of an insurance policy for you," the Colonel asked.

"Should do nicely," Ellis responded. "You do recall that I said there were two things you'd have to do to resolve this situation, right?"

"Yes. The money and the confession. I remember." With that, the Colonel rose from his desk, turned round and pulled four books from the bookcase, revealing a small safe behind it. He rotated the dial clockwise, counterclockwise, and clockwise again until the door swung open. Ellis saw the money inside, and spoke before the Colonel could take any of it out.

"Wait a minute. Sit back down."

"I thought you—"

"Just sit," Ellis said brusquely."

The Colonel sat.

I did say there were two things you'd have to do. However, the money and the confession are only one thing."

"Now see here…"

"No, you see here. I also said, you'd have to be punished for what you did."

"But—"

"Quiet!"

Unable to miss the anger in Ellis's tone, the Colonel went silent.

"We had to do something on that mission. Something to have enough strength to keep going. Something that no human being should ever have to do. But we did it. Did it to stay alive. Did it to survive. What are you willing to do, Colonel? What are you willing to do to stay alive?"

Fear gripped the Colonel. But he tried to mask it. "I'd do what any man would do. I'd do whatever it takes."

"Here's what it's going to take, Colonel. Here's what it's going to take for you to survive this night." Ellis reached down beside his chair and inside the already opened cooler he had brought with him. He pulled out a small tin tray and set it on the desk in front of the Colonel.

Then he took the lid off the tray revealing seven strips of what appeared to be fish or sushi of some sort.

"I have to apologize for the condition these are in, Colonel. They were on ice for a long time but I'm afraid I may have let them go over."

"What the hell is it?"

"You don't know?"

"I have no idea."

"Really, I thought you might have recognized him?"

"Him? What in blazes are you talking about?"

"It's your co-conspirator, Colonel. It's Henderson."

"What?"

"He's dead. And you're going to eat him."

"God, man. You're out of your mind."

"No. But Henderson probably was. And you… you have to be pretty damn sick as well to be willing to do away with human lives the way you did."

The Colonel looked down at the tray again. As he did so, Ellis spoke.

"Wondering why there are eight pieces? Here's why. One, Sanchez. He never would have died if it wasn't for you. Two, Tasso. The one who was perhaps better than all of us. Three, Adams. Good man, good soldier. Four, Devlin. A man who had dedicated himself to helping others. Five, Bevel, a woman who did absolutely nothing to deserve what happened to her. Six, Bevel's ex. Not a nice guy. But not deserving of what happened to him. Seven, Fowler. One that got away, thankfully. Eight, a Lieutenant named Carlyle, simply in the wrong place at the wrong time. But, just so you'll know, she survived too. Probably because she's tougher than any of us."

"Look," the Colonel began to plead, "I'll give you more money than I was going to give Henderson. There's more here. Right here in the safe."

"Not part of the deal, Colonel. This is something you can't buy your way out of. This is your penance, see. Your atonement for the evil that you did. You said you'd do anything to survive. And believe me, this is what you have to do. If you don't, I swear on the graves of my squad members that I will put a bullet directly into your brain pan. The time for talk's up. What's it going to be?"

The Colonel, sickened with fear and revulsion simultaneously, reached down, his hand shaking. He picked up one of the strips, held it gingerly for a moment, then closed his eyes and bit into it. An automatic gag reflex hit. His head jerked forward. He was about to spit it out when Ellis barked, "Don't you dare. Swallow it! Swallow the damn thing!"

The Colonel, holding his hand over his mouth to keep from retching, did as he was told. As he did, tears came to his eyes and rolled down his cheeks.

"Here's an idea," Ellis said, "wash that down with some of your scotch. Sure, have a drink, no sense letting good booze go to waste."

The Colonel greedily grabbed the tumbler beside the bottle, filled it with the amber liquid and took a huge swig.

"Don't waste it Colonel. You're likely to need it to finish your snack."

Eyes watering, stomach churning, bile rising in his throat. It struck the Colonel that this was the way to get through this hell. Simply throw one in his mouth, swallow it whole, then chase it with a huge drink. He could do that. He could survive. He'd show this prick of an ex-Lieutenant who a real man was. *Screw him,* the Colonel thought… *him and his gun and his ninja clothes. Screw it all. Let's do this.*

The Colonel grabbed the second piece, literally threw the thing in his mouth, swallowed hard, and quickly took a big belt of Scotch. On to the next. And the next. But on the fifth piece, Colonel Randolph Winslow Harrison threw the piece of ex-Warrant Officer Henderson too haphazardly into his mouth and it went down the wrong pipe. He gagged. He clutched his throat. He began to choke. He banged on his chest. His face turned red. His eyes blinked and bulged. Saliva slid from a mouth he was too frightened to close. He gawked imploringly, and reached his hand pleadingly across the desk at the man holding the gun on him.

Ellis had a decision to make.

CHAPTER 37

LIEUTENANT CARLYLE LOOKED DECIDEDLY BETTER than she had previously. The cast had been removed from her arm, one side of her face, while still partially bandaged, no longer had tubes or receptors attached. Her hair was combed strategically to cover most of the damage. She wore a sleek, but subtle robe belted over pajamas rather than a hospital gown. She had even applied a touch of makeup and lipstick, which she tried to convince herself was simply a return to some degree of normality rather than an attempt to look more attractive to her visitor.

Ellis had called ahead and told Carlyle he was coming. This time he was able to meet Nurse Meyers face to face and they exchanged jocular but heartfelt pleasantries before he proceeded down the hall to Carlyle's room, now absent the guard outside her door. He spoke before entering.

"Hello, everyone decent in there?"

She recognized his voice immediately. "Would it make it any difference if I said no?"

"Certainly… I'd get in there before things changed."

"Well, come on in, even if I am decent."

Ellis walked in and a smile beamed across his face like the sun streaming through her uncovered window. She was sitting in a high-back chair next to her bed. "Wow. You really look different from the last time I saw you."

"Different worse or different better?"

"The latter in spades," he responded.

"No point in me saying flattery will get you nowhere. I actually look for it wherever I can find some these days."

"My guess is you're probably finding plenty from the folks in the hospital here."

"They're paid to make patients feel better, physically and emotionally."

"Yes, well nobody's paying me and I'm saying you're definitely looking great."

She bolted right out of chit-chat into what she sensed he was feeling. "None of it was your fault, you know?"

"Nice of you to say, but—"

"No buts. I'm the one who made the decision to insert myself into your commitment. You're not to blame in any way for what happened to me. I could have done my job from a distance, just like most other lieutenants."

"But we both know you're not like most other lieutenants. I know mavericks when I see one. I mean, you're the one who told me that I'm not like most other private investigators. Two peas in a pod?"

"Sometimes it pays to be different, sometimes we're the ones paying. Occupational hazard for nonconformists, I guess."

Ellis was enjoying the give and take, but his concern for her was more important. "How's the arm? What do the doctors say?"

She forced a grin as she responded. "Aways wanted to learn how to shoot left-handed." His look must have failed the stoic test. "It's not so glum. Partial return to full use. Whatever the hell that oxymoron means. Though I'm pretty sure it doesn't mean top scores on the pistol range."

"Yeah, you say that now, but I have a feeling the Annie Oakley in you won't accept anything less. Regardless of what side you're firing from."

"Got a feeling that initially, Calamity Jane will be a more appropriate handle," she responded. "And because I know you're too gentlemanly to ask about the face, it could make a comeback they say, with the right plastic surgery. Of course, the extent needed is probably way beyond what government insurance is approved to handle. Anyway, who knows. Might look like dueling scars. Could give me some real street cred."

"As fate would have it, the poet once said, that's one thing you might not have to worry about." Then, reaching in his inside coat pocket, he pulled out a cashier's check and handed it to her. The check was made out to her in the amount of fifty thousand dollars.

"Jesus H –" she began. "Hey, I can't accept this. No way. And where the hell would you get this kind of money anyway? I don't recall seeing any trust-fund-baby notes in your 201 File."

"Who says it's coming from me? I'm just the delivery boy. Look at the address in the corner." It read:

Lieutenant Carlyle Recovery Fund
Santa Fe, Sedona, and Phoenix
Friends of Law Enforcement
(Membership Rolls Not Subject To Freedom Of
Information Act)

He never would have told her the money actually came from Colonel Harrison's safe, but before she had a chance to continue her disbelief and question him further, Ellis said, "Remember when I was here before?"

"Uh, just barely… but about this money…"

"Forget about the money. Believe me, no one's going to miss it or question where it came from. No one. But I need you to focus now. Remember, I told you about the hanger in Sedona that had Henderson's stuff and a copy of his confession in it."

"Oh, yes. I remember. Haven't looked into it yet, but—"

"Well, when you do, you'll now find a copy of a second confession in it as well. One from the guy who planned Henderson's rampage and paid him to pull it off."

"Hey, if that confession is like the one I remember from Henderson… it will more than likely never stand up in court."

"Never needs to get to a court. The fellow in the second confession has joined Mr. Henderson in Hades' waiting room."

Slack-jawed, she asked, "You didn't… did you?"

"Like Bill Clinton once said, don't ask, don't tell. The point is, you have all you need to let the appropriate authorities know what happened to Tasso, Bevel, and her ex in Santa Fe. And if you would, check with the police in Omaha about the death of an ex-private Adams. Let them know they can cross it off their books. As well as an ex-Corporal Devlin in Brookline Massachusetts. Neither place needs details. Just closure. I'm sure each will view it as one less cold case to try and keep warm."

Once more, she tried to start a question. Again, he cut her off.

"Got to run now, Lieutenant Carlyle. Still have things to do. Know you want to talk. But there will be plenty of time for that in the future. Hope we have a future. Who knows. Might be just what the doctor ordered."

With that, he kissed her sweetly on the cheek and headed for the door. Then, saying to himself, *Nothing ventured, nothing gained*, he stopped, walked back, planted a real kiss on her lips and make his exit.

She sat looking from the door to the check and back to the door again. Then she brought her hand up and let her fingers gingerly touch her lips. "God," she said out loud, "Brig Ellis, a P.I., for Christ's sake."

CHAPTER 38

ELLIS HAD RETURNED TO SEDONA with two things left to do. The first was to square accounts with Wild Bill. They met for lunch at Café Jose. With a sunset landscape on one wall, and a row of tables on the other, they sat in one of the center booths, ate Mexican food, drank Margaritas, and wrapped up their business.

Eisenstat asked, "So, you don't think there's going to be any blowback on our little adventure with animal-man, huh?"

"No," Ellis answered. "Looks like that ship has sailed and no one was at the dock to wave goodbye. My bet is the guy didn't have one friend in the world, and his employer definitely won't be raising a fuss."

"Took care of that, did you?"

"Had to be done. One way or the other."

"Which way did you choose?"

"Sometimes, you don't make the choice. Sometimes fate makes it for you."

"Yep. Fate's a bitch all right," Wild Bill said. "I'm hoping to put off meeting up with it for some time."

Ellis reached inside his jacket pocket, pulled out a sealed envelope, and handed it to Eisenstat. "Here you go. Think the cash inside will more than square us financially, but I'll always be in your debt for helping out someone you didn't even know."

"Hell," Wild Bill responded, "I knew you the first time I looked in your eyes. I said to myself, Eisenstat, those are the eyes of an upright dude. A fellow who's hard as nails on the outside, and all Boy Scout on the inside. He won't steer you wrong. And you never did."

"Can't say I was able to read you that quickly," Ellis said. "But you proved your worth. That's for sure."

"Damn, we better finish our drinks and get out of here before we wind up kissing each other."

Both men drained their glasses. Eisenstat reached in his pocket, peeled off three twenties and set them on the table under the salt shaker. "Since you gave me this," he said, holding the cash-stuffed envelope in his hand, "I should get lunch. Hope making me whole didn't put too sizable a dent in your own takeaway."

"The spoils of war are not infinite," Ellis said, but I think I have enough to take care of one last thing I have to do in Sedona."

"Oh yeah, what's that?"

"You ever buy a car back from the same person you sold it to?"

"No. But I assume it would cost you more to get it back than you made getting rid of it."

"I assume that too. Will probably take just about all I have left of the bad man's booty."

"Hope it's worth it."

"It is."

As the two were rising to leave, a flurry of activity three tables down caught their attention. A man was coughing and coughing, and couldn't seem to stop. His wife patted him hard on the back, but it didn't help. He was scrambling to his feet as he continued to choke, then all of a sudden, a sizable chunk of carne asada flew from his mouth and landed in the guacamole. He quickly grabbed a glass of water and took a huge gulp.

"Man," Eisenstat said, that looked bad, didn't it? Thought for a moment The Frontier Jew was going to have to come to the rescue. I'm highly skilled in that Heimlich Maneuver thing. You ever had to do that?"

"As a matter of fact," Ellis said, "recently."

"Really? How'd it go?"

"It didn't work."

EPILOGUE

THE FOLLOWING ITEM INITIALLY APPEARED in Virginia's Fairfax Times, a weekly newspaper whose declining advertising revenues were only outpaced by its declining subscription base. The story however, was picked up by the wire services almost immediately and subsequently graced the front pages of the country's largest printed and Internet outlets.

SENATE CANDIDATE
FOUND DEAD

Former U. S. Army Colonel and candidate for the United States Senate from the state of Virginia, Randolph Winslow Harrison, was found dead in his home yesterday. Police were called to the candidate's Fairfax residence when neighbors reported a distinctly odd smell emanating from a partially open window in one wing of the house.

Harrison's body, in a state of decay, was discovered in the library. Preliminary findings indicate the candidate had been dead for some time and was alone at the time of his death.

Authorities are stressing that there are no initial indications of foul play. When asked for comment, Investigating Officer, Vernon Tucker's only reply was "I'm guessing it was something he ate."

Ellis, back home now, was sipping coffee and reading the *San Diego Union-Tribune* with his English bulldog, Osgood, who lounged at his feet. He saw the report and said to the ponderous pooch, "You know boy, considering his public persona, they'll likely do an autopsy. Cause of death will be attributed to choking no doubt. Of course, should they closely examine the contents of his stomach, they'll likely be in for quite a surprise. Maybe even pass it on to the press. Think some intrepid reporter will want to follow up on it?"

The sturdy canine wrinkled his snout and rolled his head.

"I don't either," Ellis said. "Journalism specifically, and intellectual curiosity in general, simply aren't what they used to be."

ABOUT THE AUTHOR

JOE KILGORE has won awards for novels, novellas, screenplays, and short stories. His tales have appeared in magazines, creative journals, anthologies, and online literary publications. He is the author of *Misfortune's Wake* and *Insomniac: Short Stories for Long Nights*, as well as the Brig Ellis novels, *Fool's Errand*, *Dying Art*, *Cast Them Dead*, and *Carrion Moon*. His other novels include *The Horse Killer, A Farmhouse in the Rain*, *The Blunder*, and *The Golden Dancer*.

Prior to writing fiction, Joe had a long and successful career creating, writing, and producing television and radio commercials, plus newspaper, magazine, and internet content for an international advertising agency. He also writes novel reviews professionally for national and international firms. He lives in Austin, Texas, with his wife, Claudia, an accomplished artist. You can read more about him and his writing at JoeKilgore.com.